WOMAN

OF THE

SKY

I could but seek my own way.

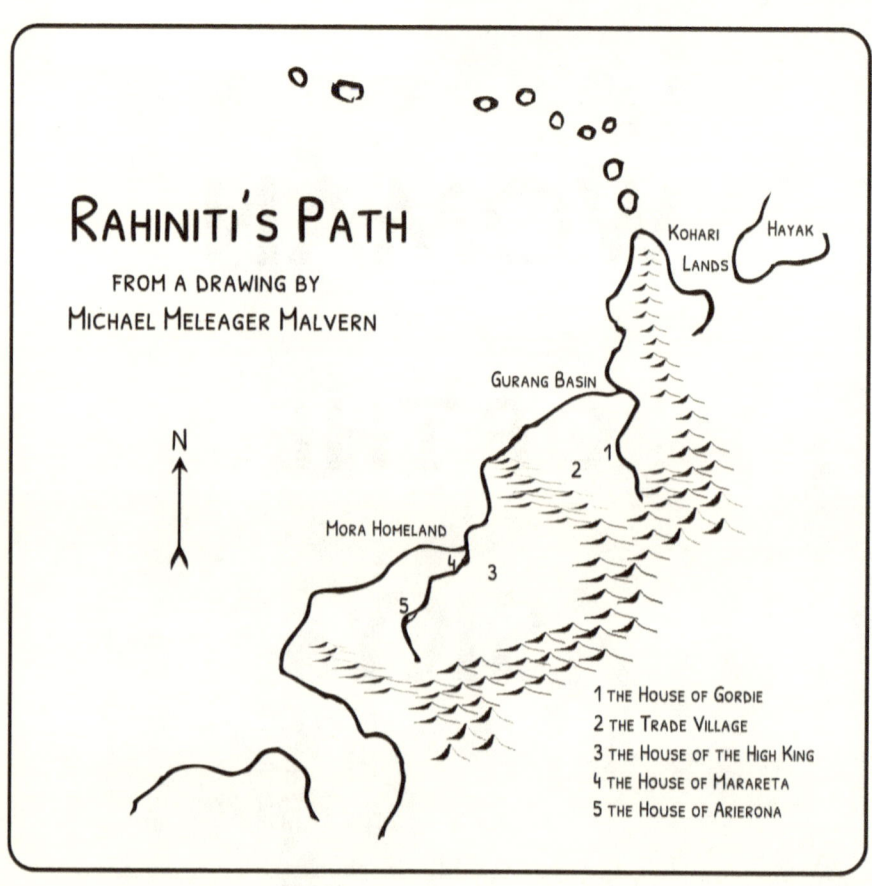

RAHINITI'S PATH

FROM A DRAWING BY
MICHAEL MELEAGER MALVERN

KOHARI LANDS HAYAK

GURANG BASIN

N

MORA HOMELAND

1 THE HOUSE OF GORDIE
2 THE TRADE VILLAGE
3 THE HOUSE OF THE HIGH KING
4 THE HOUSE OF MARARETA
5 THE HOUSE OF ARIERONA

WOMAN OF THE SKY

Stephen Brooke

Arachis Press 2018

Woman of the Sky ©2018 Stephen Brooke

ISBN   978-1-937745-50-9

Arachis Press
4803 Peanut Road
Graceville, FL 32440

http://arachispress.com

Part I. In the North

1. The House of Gordie

"Unlike others who came from the sea, I found what I wanted in this land, found it at once and chose it for myself. My wife, her people — this was enough. I could have been content."

"But you were not." I smiled up at the man by my side.

He had to laugh. "Yes, I was ambitious. *Am* ambitious, and not just for myself. I wanted what was best for the Diwarna who had taken me in and given me Demba."

Demba. Gordie had not mentioned her name in weeks. Not since the funeral.

"And now for Malee," I said.

He nodded. "Yes, for Malee." His daughter was very little yet, very young. She might not remember her mother when she grew older. Gordie stood, shielding his eyes from the sun, and peered toward the river.

I rose beside him there on his broad porch, there before the House of Gordie. "Canoes?"

"Yes." The man sighed. "I wish the only binoculars in this world weren't far away with George Bath."

I had no idea what the strange word meant or why he wanted them. Bafa, as we called him — as he called himself these days — had many odd things. And they were indeed far away, in his rooms and workshops at the House of Arierona.

Gordie reminded me of Bafa — in some ways. A little younger, but similar in height, build, coloring. I had learned the resemblance was, for the most part, a physical one. "It is Pahe, isn't it?" Two men were ascending the long slope from the river. The other was dark — a Diwarna? No. "Oh, and Bamiree."

Bamiree, as Gordie and Bafa, was one of those who had come from the sea. He dwelt among the Diwarna now, with a Diwarna wife and a Diwarna name. My people — the Mora, that is, whom I consider my people now — had called him Hare. That means 'manly' and I thought it fit him well. There was nothing to do but wait for them so I sat down again.

One could readily mistake Bamiree for Diwarna from a distance, but the differences were many close up. The muscular, broad-shouldered man stood now at the bottom of the steps, beside Gordie's second-in-command.

"Come on up," called Gordie. "What brings you here this morning, Wise?" Gordie was the only one who still used that name.

The man glanced at his companion, but Pahe only nodded toward him. "There are Kohari on the river, Cap'n." I do not know what Cap'n means. It was a joke between the two I think.

"Not unusual." Gordie took a seat on one of the woven mats and the two men joined us. "Traders?"

Bamiree shook his head. "Warriors," spoke Pahe. "But not raiders, not men out to take heads."

Then Bamiree let the real news out. "They want to speak with you."

"Ah." Gordie did not seem surprised. "We expected this would happen one day, Pahe, didn't we?"

"Yes, Lord Gordie." The half-Kohari man was as impassive as ever. I knew he disliked the Kohari, but disliked the Mora — his other half — even more. I am not sure what he thought of I who was born Kohari but became Mora!

"I am willing. Two or three envoys. No more than that." Gordie chuckled. "I am sure the Diwarna can lead them through the swamps and get them thoroughly lost."

"You could meet them at one of the villages," suggested Pahe. "There is no need for the Kohari to see your house."

One of the women of the house brought fruit and tumblers of

water. Such was customary and orders need not be given. So is it done in the houses of the Mora nobles and I had seen to it that things were the same here. There had been little discipline in the House of Gordie when I had first arrived.

"It is better that they see what I have done here, that I am not some leader of rabble, dwelling in a hut in the swamp," said Gordie.

I spoke for the first time. "It might not impress a Kohari nobleman." The house in which I had been born, the house of no one more important than a prosperous farmer, was at least as large. Or maybe it only seemed so in memory; I had left it when I was but six. "They have seen the great temple of Mihasa," I added.

Gordie seemed to be considering this, but Bamiree spoke out. "You are right, Cap'n. You need to be the lord of the manor when these men come, with warriors around you and your people working in the fields. Let them know you're here to stay."

"We both are, eh, Wise? And I'm glad of it. Most of it." Gordie paused, thinking perhaps of Demba. "My life was all laid out for me once," he continued. "I would rise in the ranks of a shipping company, the Nathan Line or another, and someday surely serve as master of my own vessel. It was a very narrow sort of destiny. I can see that now."

Much of this I did not understand but Bamiree nodded knowingly. "It's a better life for me here than the one I left behind." He rose. "I'll go back to my people —" He gave Gordie a pensive look. "*Our* people, and get it arranged. Won't need you, Pahe."

The normally taciturn warrior grinned. "I would become lost as surely as your Kohari guests."

"Even I do," admitted Bamiree. "Gordie is the only outsider who knows the swamps as well as the Diwarna themselves." He descended from Gordie's porch, and strode purposefully toward his waiting canoe.

To me, Gordie turned, saying, "I would wish you to be with us when these, ah, envoys come. You know Kohari ways better than any of us." He half-smiled. "Mora ways, too, for that matter. You could be very useful, Ranadi."

"She already is," Pahe told him, and took another slice of melon.

2. Loss

PAHE WAS AN ally of sorts. I had recognized that soon after coming to stay in the House of Gordie. Maybe I reminded him of his mother, for he had no interest in women otherwise.

Many weeks now had passed. After the wedding of my friend Teme — my best friend, I think, she had become — I decided to come north to visit Gordie and Demba. There had been a long-standing invitation, ever since Hito and I had stayed at their house, resting after our long journey over the mountains. I liked Demba and had almost not left at that time.

And I liked Gordie and their little daughter Malee and their big house on the river where everyone came and went without the ceremony of a Mora nobleman's household. I'd had enough of that for a while.

Then came the spotted fever. It did not bother me for I had contracted it as a child. Most Kohari do. Gordie said it was common, too, in the land from which he came — the land most believed was 'beyond the sea' but I knew to be another world. Knew but did not understand!

The Diwarna suffered much as it swept through their villages. For most, days of misery. Some died. Malee took sick but she was a strong girl and recovered quickly. Her father's blood, maybe. I do not know of such things. Demba tended her through her illness and I helped as I could — not with the child but by taking charge of the household.

Gordie's wife had never taken a strong hand there. It was not the Diwarna way and Demba was thoroughly Diwarna, an intelligent woman but knowing no other sort of life. Her people seem irresponsible, and maybe even lazy, to some outsiders. It is just their way of dealing with the world and better than some, I am sure.

When Demba fell ill, then I did tend her, I and Gordie, one of us ever by the Diwarna woman. Girl, I could call her; Demba was very young. Ah, we all were. For days she tossed in fevered half-sleep, knowing not who we were, where she was. She cried out for her brother Oorto, the shaman, but he was far away. For her mother, long dead but a mighty shaman in her time, Demba also called.

In the end, it was Death that came. I know not if ever I wept more, felt such loss. No, not even when I was taken from my home as a little girl to train as a temple dancer. This loss was final. My friend Demba would never sit with me again, never share her little innocent secrets. I treasure yet the memories of such moments.

And Gordie? My loss could not begin to rival his. He had never loved another. "We were children when we met," he told me, "I on my first voyage, never before away from my home, and Demba a girl of the swamps. There in the village of her people, we fell in love, and there I chose to remain — to spend my life with her."

There was little I could say to that. I only promised to stay for a time and help as I might, with his household, with Malee. He laid his wife in a grave in the hills behind his high house, though Demba's people have no funeral customs and discard their husks in the swamp.

But I spoke of Pahe, did I not? Gordie's second approved of the changes I made, of the support I gave his master when he was in need. Pahe approved of anything that helped Gordie, whom he near-worshiped. Had I thwarted my host in some way, Pahe would not have hesitated to turn against me. This I know.

Pahe — the name means 'bitter' in Kohari, but whether his mother named him so, or he himself, none know. Pahe's mother was of a Kohari trader family, it is said, widowed, who married a Mora sailor and trader. As son of such a woman, he had no place in Mora society. Here, it was different; here was the right hand of his Lord Gordie.

I give thanks to the spirit of Lord Temani'itu that he saw fit to adopt me as his daughter. Otherwise, I too, and my children — I intend to have many — would not be recognized as Mora. Oh, yes, I must thank Temani'itu's wife Hihini as well. Without her approval the old nobleman could not have named me as a member of his family.

It is good we both have been given places, Pahe and me, though I am quite without any home or wealth! My Mora friends inform me I could spend the rest of my life guesting with them, with my relatives, in truth, with any noble family. A husband would be much better, I think.

This would be my place for now. It was good to be useful. I would reside in the House of Gordie and help him as I might, take care of little Malee, continue to run his household. I would help my friend.

But had Gordie lost his own place?

3. Visitors

"Bamiree said it is better here than the land from which you came. Is it a bad place to live?"

Gordie considered this in silence for a rather long time. "For members of his, um, tribe, I think it might be. Not so for me." He laughed suddenly. "Not that I would ever want to go back!"

"Then he is of a different people than you," I said. He certainly looked different.

"Yes and no," the man replied. "His ancestors were slaves, freed now but still — well, like Pahe. Not accepted as part of our society, at least by some." He shook his head. "I never thought about that much before I came to your world."

"You were only a child," I reminded him. So Gordie had said. I considered filling my bowl again. Another serving of papaya wouldn't hurt, would it?

"Eighteen years. Yes, a child." He laughed. "And very ignorant."

"No more, my friend," was all I could answer to that. And I decided I had eaten enough breakfast.

"No. I have responsibilities now. Malee is the most important one." His eyes seemed to search for far-away things. "A messenger arrived late last night. Oorto is on his way here."

"To stay?"

Gordie shrugged. "I think not." He left it at that.

"You have other visitors to concern yourself with today," I said, rising. "And I must make myself busy too." Gordie only gave me a thoughtful look before I left him.

Couriers came and went through the morning. This was no concern of mine but I notice things. It is not as if I labored hard in the House of Gordie; there were others to do that. And the outside I left to Pahe, though I probably knew as much of managing the fields as he. Or as little!

I noticed, too, that there were more warriors about the place than was normal. Perhaps Gordie feared some treachery. Perhaps he only wished to impress his guests. Some were from the valley where many of mixed blood dwelt these days, the valley discovered by Marareta as he returned from over the mountains. Those who lived there gave a loose allegiance to Gordie though he made no claim to being their ruler. His power was here in the streams and swamps and jungles that lay between the great Gurang River and the trade village of the Mora, in the southern grasslands.

Four long canoes came up the river, our broad shallow river that joined the Gurang in a morass of swamp to our north. That entrance was hidden from the Kohari but Gordie feared they would someday discover the way. Not these Kohari, for they had been brought through winding ways by the Diwarna.

I assumed there were Kohari on those canoes. We waited on Gordie's high front porch to greet our visitors. Yes, three Kohari came up the slope with Bamiree, and over the low stone walls that stood between house and river. Noblemen — I could see that by their ornaments, their helmets, a dozen or more other little clues. They bore no tattoos to proclaim their status as do Mora nobles. As do I, these days.

One of them I recognized and was sure he recognized me. Neither of us said anything of it. Gordie and I descended the stairs to greet them.

"Cap'n, this is Habaccan," said Bamiree, indicating an older, rather ordinary looking man who had stepped forward. There was a blood-stained bandage of bark-cloth wound around his chest but no one made mention of it.

"I welcome you to my house, Lord Habaccan," spoke Gordie, "and your companions."

"We greet you, Lord Gordie," said the man. "This is Lord Hidlat." A squat, powerfully-built man with a deep scar across his face, stepped forward, respectfully nodding. He looked a true fighting man and I knew him to be one. "And Lord Mananganay," he continued. This was a young man, and tall for a Kohari.

"We come to speak with you. No more than that," said Habaccan.

"And there are many things of which we might speak," replied Gordie. "Come in and refresh yourselves. I have chambers prepared for you." He turned and led the way up the steps.

Hidlat was eying me. "Is this your wife, my lord?" he asked.

Gordie could not hide the pain this question brought him but he answered evenly. "No, Lord Hidlat." The man had an extraordinary memory for names and pretty much everything else. "My wife passed not long ago. Ranadi is assisting me these days."

"Ah." Hidlat gave me another squint. "My condolences, Lord Gordie."

"We had not heard of this," said Mananganay, in a low voice. "Any news comes roundabout to us."

"And perhaps we can change that," added Habaccan. "That is one reason we are here."

I had made certain a meal would be ready for our guests, served in a private chamber. If Gordie wished to feast them while they were here, that could come later. Bamiree surprised me by remaining, but none other of Gordie's followers sat with us. Not even Pahe.

Little of import was said. That, too, could come later. The talk did seem to keep coming around to trade and crops and that sort of thing. That was why these Kohari were here, of course, a hope of establishing peaceful trade. There is much more profit in trading with people than in trying to take their heads. Mananganay seemed to defer to the other two, for the most part, as they went on about this and that and how the kuru crop was doing, between mouthfuls of roast duck and gulps of beer.

I said little, as well, but paid attention. One thing I wondered about. "You do not have the blessings of the temple in this, do you, my lords?"

"We do not," admitted Habaccan, "but there are other cults than that of Mihasa, and there is resentment of its power and of those who serve at the great temple, those who seek to rule over all our people. Hidlat here is a devotee of Maco, with ties to her priest-hood."

The stocky warrior wiped his mouth, nodding. "She and her siblings shape all things that are, not Mihasa, who flies across the heavens each day."

Even I knew that the sun was not really Mihasa, but I assumed he was speaking figuratively. Or maybe not; the people among whom I was born are far more literal than the Mora, with their fanciful epics and legends. And I had grown up in the temple — priests do tend to be of a skeptical sort.

Gordie sat looking at the trio for a moment before saying, "Then you will have those who oppose your plans."

"Yes, my lord," agreed Habaccan. "We have enemies. They attacked our boats while we waited on the Gurang." He raised his right hand, lightly touched the bandage he wore. "We drove them off, with the help of the warrior Bamiree." The Kohari gave that man a respectful nod of the head.

"I left some of your men with them, Cap'n," said Bamiree. "I don't think anyone will give them trouble again."

Hidlat scowled. "If those were the only ones who followed us. I fear more may come."

4. Hidlat

"LORD GORDIE NAMES you 'sister,'" Hidlat said. "I do not know your true name." He had come out onto the wide rear porch, overlooking Gordie's gardens. I liked to sit there in the evening, after Malee was put to bed. Once, I sat so at the House of Temani'itu and gazed at another garden. It seemed long ago.

"Yes, Hito heard me called Ranadi in the temple and used the name. Miyawanagayun, I was once, but Rahiniti I am since I became Mora, adopted into the family of Lord Temani'itu. That is my true name now, Lord Hidlat."

Hito had also named me Tamba, 'companion,' later when we journeyed together. This lord of the Kohari need not know that.

"Rahiniti," he repeated, as if trying out the sound of it. "I do not know the Mora tongue. Does it mean something?"

"Little sky woman," I told him, "for I am small of stature, especially compared to the Mora, who tend to be a large people. And I had come down to them from the mountains, the mountains I had crossed from my homeland with the hero Hito. Sometimes I felt I was very near the sky on that journey!"

"Tales of the warrior Hito's adventure are known to us. It is probably well that my name is not mentioned in them." He took a seat on a mat near me. "How fares the man?"

"A priest now," I told him, "and with a wife."

"I am surprised that is not you."

I had to giggle. "So am I, a little! My life has been very strange among the Mora, Lord Hidlat. I am actually of higher status than Hito, having been adopted by Lord Temani'itu."

"The great admiral. High, indeed. Brother of the High King, was he not?"

"He was. I who was only a little dancer in the temple have become the friend of kings and high nobles."

"Your life has indeed been strange, Ranadi." He pondered

something for a moment. "I should address you as Lady Rahiniti, should I not?" It seemed a serious question.

I laughed. "Only if you come to visit me when I return to the Mora homeland." I would, sooner or later.

"Would that there were peace, so I might," he replied, and stared out across the garden. A single torch burnt below us, dispelling some of the deepening dusk. "Lugan stands in the east."

The evening star, the goddess of sleep — and much more. "The mountains have hidden her until now," I said.

"It is not so in my home. There she would rise from the water." He spoke this in a dialect of Kohari, not the pidgin that was the language of Gordie's house and of traders everywhere. I understood him well enough.

But I chose to continue in the pidgin. "Your lands are on the mainland, my lord?" I asked.

He shook his head. "The northern end of Hayak." This was the great isle on which Mihasa's temple complex stood, but near the other end. "Many generations ago, Mora exiles settled there and became lords of the Kohari."

"Stories tell of how they were driven from the Mora homeland. They speak of them as evil men." A sudden thought made me laugh. "As Hito once said to me, epics ever favor the winner."

Hidlat did not share my amusement. "The epics may have been right about those men, though I count them among my own ancestors." He sighed. "We did not yearn so to shed blood before they came to us."

I sat and regarded the man for a time, my knees up, my chin resting on them. "Once I thought that was the way of things," I said at last, "when I was an ignorant girl in the temple, dancing before the altar where men and women were sacrificed to Mihasa."

"Perhaps I too need spend time among the Mora," spoke Hidlat. Now it was his turn to laugh. "I could disguise myself as a trader were my ugly face not so readily recognized!"

"And Kohari traders are rarely allowed above the Great Falls," I reminded him. "But Gordie might take you to the Mora trade village to our south. We must speak of it to him." It was quite dark now. "There should be an evening meal prepared. Let us go in and see what he thinks of the idea."

The nobleman chuckled as we rose. "Lord Gordie is fortunate to have you at his side. More so, having lost his wife."

"That, my lord," I told him, "is one person I could never replace."

5. A Traitor

"MANANGANAY IS GONE," reported Pahe, practically spitting the words out. "He took a canoe and slipped away in the night."

A resigned nod from Habaccan. It was he who reported he could not find his companion this morning. "I am sorry, my friend," spoke Hidlat. So soft a voice from a man so seemingly hard! "He has betrayed you."

"Betrayed us all," came the noble's reply, "but his kinship to me makes it the more painful."

"Bamiree has already gone to scout," Pahe said. "If we're lucky, the man is lost somewhere downstream." He did not speak what we all feared — that Mananganay would find his way to the Gurang and lead invaders here.

Gordie had taken all this in without comment or evident emotion. "We should meet our enemy on the river, if we can," he now stated. "Not here. Gather a force, Pahe." He turned to me. "I wish you to take all who are not warriors to the valley of retreat. Leave no one."

He need say no more. I would see to the safety of his people at once. And his daughter!

As I turned from them, I heard a curt laugh, and Pahe saying, "Would that the Lady Teme were here to lend us her bow-arm."

"Our archers are well-trained now," came Gordie's calm voice. "We are better prepared than the last time Kohari came up the river." I heard no more for I became busy then, getting everyone organized for our march, making sure we had provisions. No matter that I did not know the way to the valley. Many here did.

We were on our path before noon, but Gordie and his warriors departed well before us, in every vessel available, canoes of many sizes and the boats their leader had ordered built. It seemed very strange to see the House of Gordie so deserted.

We met more warriors as we traveled southeastward toward our refuge, but not until the second day, for it is not a short journey. Couriers had been sent ahead, asking for aid. To the Mora trade town, as well, they had been sent, where the noble Taki kept a handful of men. If battle was to be on the river — a river, whether the Gurang or that which flowed by Gordie's house — they would be far too late to take part. But if Gordie did not win victory on the water, they would be needed when he fell back. If fall back he could.

"Maybe our lord should move his house," Malee's nurse said to me as we walked along, taking turns carrying the child. "It would be safer to live in the valley."

I thought maybe she was right, but it would take him too far from the Diwarna of the swamps, those he considered his adopted people. Too, it would take him away from the profitable trade on which he depended. None of this I said. My thoughts were on what might be happening behind us, where warrior would be facing warrior in a battle to the death.

To the death, for they could not allow any Kohari who knew the hidden way escape. Truly, it would be best if they caught the Kohari on the Gurang, before that way into the river was learned. Then maybe only Mananganay would have to die.

I am not eager to see men die. Not Gordie's men. Not the Kohari, though they are no longer my people. Certainly not Lord Hidlat, who had saved Hito and me from death. Or death for Hito, anyway, and life as a concubine to the odious Bohasuk for me.

Not until the third day did we reach our destination, resting in rough, open — and crowded — shelters that had been built along our path. And it was uphill all the way! A broad, pleasant valley it was, nestled in the foothills, a clear, fresh stream rushing and rollicking through it. This was the path Marareta and his companions had followed on their way down from the mountains and a few of those companions dwelt here now.

I know not the names of trees but they stood tall and straight on the slopes. Below, cleared fields held crops of millet and kalina, and many sapa trees were planted about the houses. These grow quickly and their bark is used to make cloth. In the lands of the Mora, that is; the Kohari prefer the bark of the kuru tree. I think it might be too cool in that valley to grow kuru.

But that mattered little to me right then. First, I must get my people — my people? Perhaps they were, at least for the time. I must get my people settled. And ever in the back of my mind was concern for Gordie and his warriors. I suppose that was in all our minds.

None the less, I slept well in a real house that night.

6. The Valley

HITO HAD BEEN one of those who accompanied Marareta across the mountains and back, years ago. Thrice had the warrior crossed, more than any other man, and the last time with me. We did not come by this way then.

I thought on Lord Hidlat's words. It would not have been strange were I wife to Hito now. I still could be. A second wife, it is true, but the Mora often have more than one spouse. The women too! That is more common among the nobles than the commoners, for it is often about alliances and property.

Hito was seen as noble now, having married the noblewoman Mehetu. I liked Mehetu. Her son, Toare, I liked as well. He was much smitten with me when he was younger but was long over that. Or seemed to be. The boy had the makings of a great bard, it was said, and studied with Master Ulani. I found myself missing my friends in the Mora homeland. Had it not been for the death of Demba, I would have returned by now.

A place such as this valley was not for me. Nor was the simple life Hito now led as a priest. Ah, not so simple, I suppose, for important men sought his advice and he often was not to be found in the little hut at the shrine of Teva.

Now those I led here were settled, there was little to do but wait for news. Lanada they named this valley, meaning 'place of the path' in the pidgin. It *was* another way for those who chose to live here, not Mora nor Diwarna nor Kohari, but a path of their own to follow. Not that all who lived in Lanada were of mixed blood. Some were spouses of such men or women; some only sought freedom and a new life, for one reason or another. It was best not to ask questions of them.

Nor to assert myself myself here. My task had been to bring Gordie's people. Others could tend to them now, the headman these settlers had chosen, his deputies. So I rested in one of the long houses and watched the day pass.

Someone sat down beside me on the worn grass mat. A glimpse sidelong — a Diwarna woman I did not know. I paid her no more attention. I paid nothing much attention for some time.

"You are a friend of Hito, are you not?" she asked eventually.

I turned toward her now. "I am. You know the warrior?"

She nodded. "I, as you, crossed the mountains with him. His first time. I am Amlee."

Ah. Tala's partner in the making of pottery. That skill they had brought back with them from the great Valley of Visions that lay beyond the peaks. Amlee had never seemed to be at the trade village when I visited.

But that was only twice, so it meant little. "I am, um, Ranadi," I replied. Maybe I should have used my Mora name but Ranadi came first to my lips. "Do you live here, Amlee?"

"No, but my man does. He, too, was one of those who followed Marareta." Her smile was rueful. "But first we followed the traitor Nezama."

I knew the tale. The bards sang it. "Lord Gordie has invited us to live and work at his compound," she continued. "I might. It would be closer to my people."

"Surely not Tala," I said.

"No. She has no time for our pots anymore, since marrying Taki and helping him run things at the Mora village." Again, her smile held a suggestion of regrets. "Neither of us handles clay much anymore. We have taught others the skill."

Soon that skill would spread everywhere. The Mora had long made crude earthenware vessels — yes, I had seen the misshapen bowls — but their skill with basketry and wood carving had meant little interest in pottery making. That changed when these two unknown women had brought home new techniques.

"I am sure Gordie would be able to sell all the pots you make for him," I told her. "Maybe to the Kohari." Trade on the Gurang, rather than war. I knew that was what the man wanted.

23

"The Lord Gordie is ambitious," Amlee allowed. "Perhaps too ambitious."

I had to agree. "Perhaps." It might all have come to an end already. There was no word yet on battle won or lost, or even joined. We could only wait.

What of Malee if things went wrong? I decided right then that I would take her back to the Mora homeland. Oorto, her uncle, and Lord Marareta would know what was best for the child. But I should not be killing off Gordie before I heard any news!

And Oorto was on his way here. I was forgetting that. Something rubbed against my leg. "Aiee! What —?" Oh, it was a cat, small and gray. I had never seen one until my first visit to the trade village. These, too, the woman beside me and her friend had carried back from beyond the mountains. "They are here, too?" I asked. I was not certain I liked the little animals.

The Diwarna woman picked up the creature. It did make a pleasant sound as she stroked its fur. "They are useful," she declared. "They hunt the little furry thieves that would eat our grain."

"Not when they lie sleeping in your lap."

"Ah, but you see," said Amlee, "there is not one mouse on me!"

7. Victors

"Lord Gordie is coming here," the courier informed us. "He said to tell you that he is safe and nothing more."

Koaoba, headman of Lanada, made a low sound that might be interpreted as disgust. "That is like Gordie."

I shrugged. "So we wait." I didn't feel like walking back to his house right then, anyway. "How soon?" I asked the messenger.

"They departed even as I did," he reported, "but would not travel so quickly. Tomorrow, I would think." The man hesitated. "One of the Kohari lords travels with him."

"The ugly one?" I asked, smiling. I suspected it would Hidlat.

"Indeed, my lady. The older man was hurt in the battle." He looked uncomfortable, of a sudden. "I should not have told you that."

"We won't let Gordie know," Koaoba told him. "You know where the food is." That was his only dismissal but the courier took his cue and went looking for a meal and, most likely, a bed. "I do not like the thought of any Kohari warrior coming here," the chieftain said to me.

It did seem odd. Gordie must trust Hidlat more than I would. "Assuming he also leaves," I replied. I didn't really mean it but it would give the man something to think upon.

I didn't think about it at all. Gordie's doings were his own business. It was near dusk the next day that his party came trudging up the valley. "Your daddy is coming," I whispered to little Malee, half-asleep in my arms.

"Mommy?" she murmured. I had no answer for that. She would forget, in time. I was a bit older when last I saw my mother and can not recall her face.

Yes, Hidlat came with the handful of men. I could spy the squat nobleman flanked by Bamiree and a pair of Diwarna, four of Gordie's retainers. Not Pahe — he would be in charge back at the house. Those Diwarna were unlikely to have taken part in any fighting. It is not their way to do battle, but many a Kohari raider has fallen to a spear launched from the cover of swamp or jungle.

And their master, their Lord Gordie, strode at the fore. He was the sort of man who would think to do so when making an entrance. For all that Gordie was a good man — or so I believed — he was also a calculating one.

But there was no calculation when he took Malee into his arms. "I thank you," he said to me, "for seeing my daughter and my people to safety. Greetings, Koaoba," he went on, turning to the man. "We are weary and we hunger. Might we ask lodging of you and yours?"

Very diplomatic, I thought. Another way the man was alike to Lord Bafa. "You are always welcome, Lord Gordie," replied the headman. "A meal has been prepared."

Gordie gave the man a half-smile, little more than a twist of one corner of his mouth, and asked, "And would I be welcome if I moved here permanently, I and all my people?" Koaoba seemed to be looking for an appropriate answer — unsuccessfully — when Gordie laughed. "I have been advised to do so, once or twice. I think I am not yet ready to run from the Kohari." But the implication was there that he might someday, that it might prove necessary.

"Today they ran from us," Bamiree put in. "Those that yet lived."

I fell in beside Hidlat as we proceeded toward the long house of the headman. "Is Lord Habaccan badly hurt?" I asked him.

"No, my lady. He but reopened his earlier wound, over-exerting himself." The Kohari snickered. It sounded like a snicker, anyway. "I tell him he is too old to charge into battle!"

"And, ah, Mananganay?"

"Dead. We shall speak of such things later." A dismissal, but a polite one. Hidlat was most certainly accustomed to giving orders and having them followed. Especially by women! It was not the way of Kohari women to be forward, to ask questions as had I, but I had picked up Mora ways, considered myself Mora. I have said this before, have I not?

Others have picked up such ways, as well. As in the House of Gordie, the meal was served in the Mora fashion, laid out on a long mat on the floor, feasters lined up on both sides. But men and women mingled here, which was not the Mora way. In the house of a Mora noble, all the women would be to the left of the host, the men to the right.

I am told the Diwarna ever sit in circles when they share a meal. I would have liked to visit one of their villages some day. But I was here, in the valley named Lanada, on this day. It was not surprising that talk soon turned to the battle.

"We caught them near the mouth of the river," said Gordie. "The traitor —" He gave a quick glance at Hidlat and then away. "Apparently noted enough landmarks to lead them there."

"Who knows whether they could have found their way through the swamp?" added Bamiree.

"That was not a chance we could take." Gordie sighed. "I would rather we could have slain them all."

Bamiree said something in a language I did not recognize and laughed rather unpleasantly. Gordie gave a sober nod. "An old saying in our homeland — 'dead men tell no tales,'" he told us.

Koaoba took a long draft from his bowl of beer before observing, "I think some version of that is known in all lands."

"And always good advice," spoke Hidlat. "We did what we could. Now let the gods decide what will be."

Gordie made no answer to that but I knew him to be a man who worshiped no gods. It was whispered he did not believe they existed.

"Did your men take part in the battle, Lord Hidlat?" I asked.

"No. The Diwarna had guided our boats to a hiding place in

the swamp. The men saw nothing of the battle nor even knew it was taking place."

Bamiree chuckled. "They would not even be able to find their way back to the Gurang, I fear, if the Diwarna left them there."

"But they will not," added Gordie. "I sent word to lead them back to the river, as the danger has passed." He paused, introspective, for a moment before adding, "For now."

Hidlat toyed with a bowl of sapa fruit, before looking up. "Those were of my people," he said. "Enemies, yes, and we Kohari are ever at war with each other. Yet — to see them destroyed so. They had no chance, did they, Lord Gordie?"

"I —" Gordie for once seemed at a loss for words. For a moment only. "I wasn't sure when we headed to battle, Hidlat. The last Kohari incursion I fought we defeated, yes, but it was not so easy a victory. And had there been more warriors against us, more boats, it might have been different this time."

Bamiree snickered. "Yes, let's face three to one next time instead of just twice our number."

Hidlat had to smile, a bit grimly, at that. "Your boats are better. Your archers are better. And those sideways bows —"

"Crossbows, we call them," interjected Gordie.

"Crossbows. They are deadly."

"Yes, they are," Gordie agreed. He squinted, concentrating for a moment before speaking further. "You saw many of the smaller ones. Those we made first and fitted to all the boats, for they allow men to shoot while mostly remaining hidden."

"Yes, an archer with a normal bow must stand and expose himself."

"Exactly so. Then we recognized that they could be made larger and heavier. Heavy enough to put a bolt through a boat."

"The cap'n recognized it," spoke Bamiree. "All this was his idea."

"Some of it," admitted Gordie, "but Lord Bafa first suggested crossbows to me." He gave me a questioning look. "You know Bafa, don't you?"

"Quite well," I admitted. I was not about to say we were lovers for a time. In a Mora gathering it might be different. "He has married my best friend."

"Oh, Teme. Yes. They were both here at the same time. Together but not yet *together*. Now she," said Gordie, "is the best archer you might ever hope to see, Lord Hidlat."

"Or not see, maybe!" I added.

Hidlat looked skeptical of the whole idea of a woman warrior but said naught. Instead, he asked, "Were those, um, spears on the front of your boats also your idea, my lord?"

"Well, Pahe gave me the idea. He noted that our boats were built so sturdily we could punch right through your light Kohari craft. So I had the rams added to them. They did work rather well, didn't they?"

"They did," agreed the Kohari noble. "But it was an unexpected tactic."

"And the next time they might know well enough to get out of the way, eh?" Gordie laughed. "I guess I shall just have to come up with something else!"

8. Grasslands

"I HAVE SENT word to Taki that Oorto should await us at the trade village," said Gordie. "I would like for you to see it, Hidlat."

The Kohari but shrugged. "I have heard of this place. Is it far?"

"No further than my house," came the reply. "I shall ask Bamiree to escort my people back there." Gordie turned his head to me. "But you I would ask to accompany us."

I had no objection. Oh, but — "What of Malee?"

An introspective look from Gordie. "I was considering leaving her here. She would be safer."

That would not do! The girl should be with her father, not abandoned among strangers. I suppose my face betrayed my feelings. "Or bring her along with us," Gordie laughed. "Malee might as well see her Uncle Oorto."

My thought had been to send her home with her nurse but this would be even better. Maybe the nurse should come too. "Amlee and some others from this valley will travel with us," he added. "They do carry trade goods there and back regularly."

Gordie gazed southwestward, more or less the direction we would take. "Once, I thought nothing of traveling the way from Diwarna lands to the village by myself. Things have changed. Men are seen where they have no reason to be. Mora men, it is reported." Seeming to speak as much to himself as anyone else, he stated, "My own success might play a role in that."

"You must make yourself master in this land or others will take what you have," asserted Hidlat. "That would be best for all, for your people, for the Kohari and the Mora, to have a strong ruler here with whom we can deal."

"I suppose so," admitted Gordie. Then he gave me a wink. "Ranadi here is attempting to turn me into a noble Mora." Hidlat grimaced but said nothing. Maybe he thought Gordie should be a noble Kohari instead.

"We shall depart in the morning. I am sure you and Bamiree

can sort things out. I must do business with our host." With that, the young man left us. Man — what else might I call him? He had no noble title among any people, even if his followers did address him as 'Lord.' Gordie might have claimed no other title than 'trader,' which he was, certainly, successful and wealthy in goods.

Men drifted into Lanada all the day, warriors who had gone to the House of Gordie when called. Things were returning to normal, and I busied myself with preparing for departure. Malee's nurse I chose to send home with the others. I could take care of the girl during our side-trip to the Mora trade village.

Mora in name — Gordie essentially ruled there too, the official representative of the High King being a man of his own choice. He seemed willing to leave things so.

At dawn we left, or before dawn truly, for the sun was only a rumor of light behind the mountains. Gordie's four warriors accompanied us, and five Lanadans, one a woman. These latter all had enormous pack-baskets strapped to their backs, full of whatever they hoped to trade at the village.

We followed a clear, well-used pathway, traveling more west than southwest, downward toward the savannas that lay between hills and jungle. Here, as on the way between the valley and his house, Gordie's men had erected rough shelters, for it was a journey of days. Hidlat marveled at the grasslands when we reached them, wide rolling expanses with but the occasional tree raising its branches to the azure overarching skies. There are no such lands within the Kohari realms.

It was near dark on the second day. "A shelter is not much further," one of the men of the valley assured us. "We should push on to it."

"It is a clear night," I objected. "Why not camp right here?" I was tired of walking. Tired of carrying a fussy Malee as well.

All looked to Gordie for a decision. I suppose he was used to that. "A little longer," he said. "Not if it gets too dark."

It was already too dark for me. A whistling sound, of a sudden. A thud and one of the men spun and fell to his knees, gripping a shoulder. "Sling!" shouted someone. "Over there," came another voice.

Amlee had gone to the downed man. He seemed all right but I was more concerned about the child I was holding. I hunkered on the pathway, shielding her as best I could.

As for Gordie's warriors, two immediately attempted to shield him, as well, while the other pair rushed toward the direction of our assailant. The presumed direction; who could be certain in the dark? Gordie impatiently pushed his protectors aside. "Any sign?" he called.

"No, my lord," came an answer. "He must have run at once."

Hidlat stood with his flint-edged sword in hand. "That man was standing beside you, Lord Gordie," he pointed out. "I would think you were the intended target."

There were murmurs, mostly suggesting agreement with this. "Not one of your Kohari enemies, surely," said Gordie. It seemed unlikely one would be here, so far from the Gurang — their only access to this land.

"Maza's shoulder is broken," announced Amlee, putting an end to the conjecturing. "We need to get him to shelter."

Gordie nodded. "Let's move on," he said, "and reach a place where we can rest. I think it has grown too dark for any more slung stones."

And maybe darkness was all that kept a would-be assassin from hitting his mark.

9. The Trade Village

ONE MIGHT GUESS that many questions were asked once we settled around a fire. A small fire, for wood is scarce on the savanna. Those questions had to remain unanswered.

"We must be more cautious from now on," spoke a warrior.

Another said, "But it is open ground between here and the village, and we should be there by tomorrow evening."

"Best we hurry on tomorrow, then," spoke Gordie. "So sleep well." With that he lay himself down; soon so did we all. That is not to say we all found sleep at once. I know I lay and looked at the numberless stars for a time, listening to little Malee breathing beside me. Who would wish to slay Gordie? I wondered.

Many. I knew this. Not just Kohari. There were Mora who feared his growing power to the north of their homeland. There were those who lived here who might wish to rival him or take his place. Even among those who served Gordie, perhaps. I had learned, dwelling in the temple of Mihasa, to trust no one. It was a place of petty rivalries, constant intrigues. And I had taken part in them as much as any, yes, and played better than most.

I was not that person anymore, was I? That ignorant, self-centered girl who scarce know right from wrong — I had left bits of her behind as I traveled to this day, left them in the high, cold mountains, by the Great Falls, in the House of Temani'itu and by the shores of sacred A'auwa. And if I hadn't quite rid myself of all that was Miyawanagayun, so be it. There was enough of Rahiniti now. I fell asleep with that thought.

We did travel quickly the next day. As quickly as possible with our laden traders from the valley — with my short legs, I was happy with the pace they set. It was little past mid-afternoon when we reached the small bowl-shaped valley, set among the rolling hills of the savanna, where stood the trading village. One building rose above all else there, a true, high-roofed Mora house.

Most of the rest were no more than huts, many used for storage rather than as residences.

Hidlat did not seem impressed. "The Mora lands lie how much further?" he asked, looking in somewhat the proper direction.

"Two days journey, if one hurries," I said. "That brings one to the hills marking their northern border."

"I would like to stand on those hills and look upon the Mora homeland someday."

Once I had done so. I am afraid the view was not very impressive. "We could claim you are a prisoner of war we have made our slave," I told him. "There are many so scattered across Mora lands."

The Kohari frowned. "I do not like the thought of my people in captivity."

"Most are freed after a time. Many choose to remain."

"And take Mora wives, more often than not," added a warrior standing near us. He chuckled, yet his next words were tinged with sadness. "There is always a surplus of widows."

"Yes," I said. "It is considered a fair exchange — war took their husbands away, war gave them new ones."

Hidlat slowly shook his head. "Mora customs are strange." Kohari kept only the heads of men they captured.

To the House of the Mora we made our way. It was not a great house, not one to rival Gordie's nor that of any important Mora noble, but it was erected on the same plan, post and beam, mats for walls and a thatched roof atop. The timbers needed to be brought from a considerable distance, for no large trees grew near. "We must see to Maza first," stated Gordie. The injured man stood impassively, his arm in a makeshift sling of bark-cloth. "Amlee?"

"Already gone," reported a warrior. All the laden traders from Lanada had disappeared, off to attend to whatever business they had, or maybe just to find beds and meals. There were open communal huts for the use of travelers and traders, and food was always made available.

Food largely provided by Gordie, these days. "Then we shall let Tala take charge," said he. "Come." We ascended to the high porch of the Mora house. One could survey much of the village from there.

It was perhaps not surprising that Amlee was already with her friend and business partner. She and Tala came forth. "Welcome, Lord Gordie. My husband has not yet returned from your house." Her eyes went to Maza. "This is the injured man? Why don't you get him inside? There are rooms prepared for all of you." Tala's serious demeanor gave way to a smile. "And a friend waits too."

I do not know if she hadn't noted me — I am small, admittedly, but not that small — or if Tala wished to attend to other business first. Her eyes went to me and then to the little one I carried. "We welcome you as well, Lady Rahiniti." With that, she turned and led the way in.

"Oorto is here?" I asked. Surely that was who she meant.

"He is." A sigh. "The death of Demba weighs on him."

"On all of us." But more on her brother and her husband, undoubtedly. This woman, too, had been her friend. And what of Amirea, far away at the House of Arierona? The news must have reached her by now, the news of her best friend's passing. It was good that she had been able to make the journey here the past year, to visit a last time, though neither had known this.

Down the entrance hall we passed, into the central chamber. The flicker of stone lamps dispelled but a little of the darkness; an acrid odor wafted from them, quite different from that of the sweet coconut oil that would be burning across the hills in Mora houses. "A meal will be prepared," Tala announced. "I leave you to the attendants now."

And so we came that evening to the trade village of the Mora, and the House of the Mora that stood in its midst, weary of our journeying.

10. In the Dark

"Poneiva asked that I bear messages to you," said the slender shaman. "Those can wait till the morrow." His attention returned to the little girl in his lap, eating bits of melon from a wooden bowl.

That the High King would have words for Gordie surprised me not at all. Poneiva had spoken to me before I came to visit, but only asking that I be observant and tell him all things I noted when I returned. Yes, to be a spy!

I had forgotten most of that, with all that had happened. Watching Malee reminded me of something else. "Tala," I spoke, "do you not have a child now?" She had been pregnant when I passed through earlier, and reports had reached us of a son.

"He sleeps," she replied, her voice soft. "We could go and peek at him if you wish." That idea was momentarily forgotten when a bustle arose down the hallway. "Ah, my husband has come home!"

A moment larger, an extremely large Mora man sauntered in. Many Mora are tall but few as tall as Taki. That he was fat too is not so important. "Your largest child," I joked. He looked back and forth between the two of us, wondering why we laughed.

Only for a moment. "Lord Gordie. I welcome you to my house." Taki was a noble and had the manners of one. His eyes swept along the line of men seated to Gordie's right, then returned to Hidlat.

"This is Lord Hidlat," said Gordie. "I assume you met my other Kohari guest."

Taki nodded, his face betraying no feelings one way or another about such guests. "I will cleanse myself and join you," he said, and hurried into the hall to his left, the one which led to his and Tala's rooms.

"I have heard of this man's fighting prowess," spoke Hidlat.

I couldn't help but tell him, "Yet Hito rubbed his face in the dirt when they wrestled." This I do not think Tala appreciated.

And memories of Hito came flooding back into my mind.

What adventures we shared! Ah, more than adventures — he was my first love. I just might marry him yet, I decided.

Taki was not alone when he returned to us, but carefully carried a small bundle in his arms. "He was awake," he told Tala, somewhat apologetically, handing the infant down to her and taking his place at the head of those gathered. Here, in this house, he took precedence over Gordie; officially, he no longer served the man who once was his master but held this post directly from the High King. Never mind that he still deferred to Gordie in most things.

I leaned in to see the little boy. A handsome child, healthy, and nursing vigorously. "What name has he?" I asked.

Tala smiled at her large husband. "Taki insisted we name him Hito."

My surprise must have been evident. "I owe Master Hito for setting me on the road that led me here," Taki said. "And for being my friend when I had none."

"I might say the same," I told him.

Hidlat, silent through most of our meal, spoke. "Hito, I think, owes as much to you as you to him."

"So the epics say," agreed Taki. He squinted at the man. "They speak also of a lord of the Kohari who aided him."

"That warrior should remain nameless," responded Hidlat.

Neither Hito nor I had ever hesitated to name Lord Hidlat in our tales, even if he hadn't made it into any poems. Perhaps I would be more circumspect from now on.

"That you came to my house can not remain hidden," said Gordie.

Hidlat shrugged. "There will be rumors. They will not matter. But," he continued, "helping one escape from the altar of Mihasa would be a much graver charge."

I nodded. "That is so."

All were weary. All soon left for their sleeping chambers. Even

Gordie, who might have talked all night had any been willing to remain awake. Malee slept in my room, but no other.

I know not how long I had slept when a voice, low, awoke me. I started but at once realized it was Oorto. "Something is happening in this house," he whispered. "I came first to be certain you were safe." Probably Malee more than me, I thought, not that it mattered any.

"I have heard things that do not sound right," Oorto continued. His ears, the ears of a swamp-bred Diwarna, were more discerning than those of most. More than mine, for sure. "Remain here and be on guard." With that he slipped out.

Why come to our room? Maybe because of Malee, maybe because his chamber adjoined. I carried no weapon, no, not even a knife. Little good it would do for me to be on guard! But I gathered up the sleeping girl, ready to protect or to run, if need be.

I peeked into the hall. As in most Mora houses, the room was open; some hang mats or bark-cloth in their entryways, others do not care. That is the Mora way. I have tried to be nonchalant about this lack of privacy but it is hard.

Shouts, from somewhere in the direction of the common room. Someone running my direction? It was hard to tell in the dark. I stepped back into the room, rocking little Malee to keep her quiet, as a body rushed by. Which direction it was going, I am not sure.

A light. Torches must have been lit, somewhere. A form silhouetted. Two forms, rather. "Lady Rahiniti?" That was Hidlat's voice.

"Here," I called. "What has happened?"

The man beside him, one of Gordie's warriors, held a small lamp. I could see the Kohari's sword in his hand and I could see the blood on its jagged flint edges. "Assassins. Three we slew. Some say there was another. Did anyone pass here?"

"In the dark, yes. I could not see who it was." I stared at the man. "Did they seek your life?"

He spat out only, "Not me."

"It was Lord Gordie they attacked," said his companion.

11. Oorto's Message

"HAD THOSE MEN known where I slept it might have been different," stated Gordie. "They had to search for me."

Hidlat glared at Taki. "Your servant has been lax." The big man shifted uncomfortably on his feet.

"Not my servant. My host. Taki is the representative of the High King here." In name — this we all knew. Well, perhaps not Lord Hidlat. Gordie went on. "I should have said something of the earlier attack."

"This has happened before, has it not?" I asked. I half-remembered some story.

"In the time of Lady Pua," replied Gordie. "A priest attempted to assassinate her. Sent by the rebels, it was assumed." He paused for a couple seconds, perhaps searching through memories. "Marareta was in the village but it was Neatanu who was here and killed the intruder."

This I did not know. "He is an old man," was all I could think to say.

Gordie chuckled. "And as many old men, he slept lightly. That was fortunate." He nodded amiably toward Oorto. "It is fortunate too that Diwarna sleep lightly."

The shaman only returned the acknowledgment, but more gravely.

"At least one of those slain was a Mora commoner," said Taki, seeking perhaps to shift the conversation. "The other two — it is hard to say. Men of mixed blood, maybe."

Gordie gazed out over the village, awakening now with the dawn. "It is easy for men of any sort to come and go here unnoticed. That can not be changed."

I too looked at the trade village, laid out below our place on the high porch. It was shrouded in the mists of morning, which often gathered in this little bowl of a valley. The lake at the north end could not be seen through the fog. Men and women were starting to move about, some finding breakfast, some claiming the best spots in the marketplace to lay out their trade goods. Lord Gordie was right — the existence of this village depended on traders being able to move freely.

"But it wouldn't hurt for the noble Taki to post an extra guard or two here in his house," I said.

Taki agreed with this. "This is so, Lady Rahiniti," he answered at once. "I have a family to protect now."

"But I don't matter that much, eh?" Gordie asked, and then laughed loudly at Taki's expression. "Have no fear, my friend. I understand your feelings completely."

Family — Gordie's own little Malee came first for him now, was all he had left. I think we all understood that. I rose. "I should go tend to Malee," I announced, "and maybe find something to eat."

"Yes," agreed Gordie. "Let's get out of this damp." The rest followed him into the House of the Mora, but I left them, heading for Tala's chambers. Malee was there, tended by little Hito's nurse.

The girl was awake and had attention for nothing but the baby, delighted by this new play thing. "Eeto!" she told me, as I entered. "'E's *my* baby." She was speaking more every day, was she not? Malee had become withdrawn after her mother's death but that seemed to be changing.

"I am not sure what Tala might think of that," I said. "She might want Hito back one of these days."

Malee considered that. "That's all right, Ranadi. She's Eeto's mommy." And then the tears began.

What to do? I knew little of children, in truth. I let her into my arms and whispered, "Let us go find your daddy."

All were in the central common room, breakfasting on dried fruit and cold yams. Malee went to her father at once, nestling on his lap, as I took a place to the left of Tala. Again, my rank was higher — much higher — but as lady of the house, as hostess, she had the place above me. They did keep to Mora custom in such things here, though not so rigorously as those who had been here before, Ma'are and her husband Heho. To them, raising their children as Mora was nearly an obsession, to the point where they would allow no other language be spoken in the house.

We, however, were conversing in the pidgin. I had a fleeting thought that it would not be a bad idea for Malee to learn Mora, before my attention went to what was being discussed. "I wanted you here before I listened to Oorto's message, Ranadi," spoke Gordie. "You know both the Mora and the Kohari as few others." He turned to the shaman without further words.

"I am no official courier to recite another's words," said Oorto. "Nor do I serve the Mora. I but bear Poneiva's invitation to visit him at the House of the High King."

"To discuss our future." Gordie nodded. "I might do this." He turned his eyes to Hidlat. "As I have been discussing it with others."

"You know we would rather you not forge closer ties with the Mora," said the Kohari nobleman. "That was, in part, why we came. Many fear your combined power would shut us out of the Gurang. Out of all the south."

"And many among the Mora have similar fears," Gordie said. He turned his attention back to Oorto. "What would keep Poneiva from taking me captive if I entered the Mora homeland?"

"The High King knew that might be a concern. He has sworn an oath that you will have free passage in his lands."

Gordie thought on this for only a moment. "Empty words from some, but I trust you, my brother. Yet" he said, "there are other Mora who might not feel bound by such an oath. Mahutunoa mistrusts my intentions, I know."

"He fears his kingdom will no longer control the only route across the hills," Taki stated. "I hear this from traders who come here."

To this Hidlat added, "And who can say who sent those assassins?"

"The more reason to speak with Poneiva," decided Gordie. "I shall visit him. Soon." He looked at Malee and me. "I wish you to remain here with my daughter while I prepare, Ranadi. We'll all go across the hills."

12. The Marketplace

"I would be tempted to take you home as a third wife," said Hidlat, "but I know you would never accept."

No, I would not, though this Lord of the Kohari was a good man, a wealthy and powerful man, and a great warrior. I was Mora now and that was the world in which I belonged. I was no longer Miyawanagayun nor even Ranadi.

"I think your first two wives would not not like it."

"They would fear you!"

I said nothing of the fact that the priests of Mihasa would want my head if ever I were to return to the Kohari realm. I like it where it is. So I but laughed.

We wandered the marketplace of the Mora village, with no intentions other than to walk and see things. Hidlat would leave at dawn on the morrow, back to the House of Gordie and then to his home on Hayak, to rule as a lord of the Kohari. It was unlikely I would ever see his homely face again. A face I liked, a face grown familiar.

Hidlat had claimed to follow Maco, goddess of storm, had he not? A deity fit for a warrior, all striving and movement. She and her sister goddess Lugan are the two halves of creation, balancing energy and rest, while their husband Lacu provides the time for them to act in our world. Once I had seen Lugan, the star of evening and morn, as my patroness — all dancers did, truly — but had not thought of such things in a long time.

Hito served a comfortable god at his shrine by A'auwa, Teva, a god of love and gentle rain, a god of fertility and family. Not for me, I knew. If I honored any god it was all-encompassing Rai. After all, was I not named for him?

Hidlat watched another barrow go by. He had never seen such before; indeed, there were few elsewhere so far as I knew. The man who first built one had a workshop here somewhere. I should take this Kohari noble there, I decided.

Dutsa he was called. As Gordie and Marareta, he was one of those who came to us from the sea. Many called him Master now, or even Taona. I never completely understood just what taona meant; maybe one must be born Mora to truly grasp some nuances of their language. I did know his shop lay in the southeastern corner of the village and needed only ask directions once.

Dutsa was a stocky man, nearly as much so as Hidlat but without the warrior's lean muscles. Pale, he was, but his face was red from exertion, where not covered by a thick beard. We found him in an open hut, tools and stacks of bamboo and what seemed trash to me — but probably was not — scattered about. Dutsa was ordering a young assistant to carry out some task. The words made little sense to me.

"Yes, Master Gaho," replied the boy and hurried off.

"Gaho?" I asked. "'The clever one?'" I translated the Mora name into the pidgin for Hidlat's sake.

"I am not clever at all. Just a simple craftsman," he claimed. The man seemed slightly embarrassed by the name. "Some have taken to calling me that."

"You must be clever to create such wonders," averred Hidlat. The man was impressed, though not inclined to show it.

"I'm just recreating things that were common where I came from, sir," replied the craftsman. "And it was not that I actually knew how to make these things. Just that I knew it could be done! Then it was only a matter of figuring out how." He gazed about the hut. "I leave the inventing to others. Some of these young fellows that help me have come up with ideas I would never have thought of."

"But you planted the seeds," I told him.

"I suppose so, um, Ranadi, isn't it?"

"It might as well be," I replied. "This is Hidlat." There was no point in saying 'Lord.' This man was never one to use titles. Maybe he did not even realize Hidlat was Kohari — none had ever come to

45

this village before. Any Mora would recognize his nationality by his bowl-cut hair, if naught else.

"Well, welcome both to my workshop. Need a barrow?"

"I would that I could take one home with me," answered Hidlat. He examined one, perhaps thinking to attempt reproducing the design. "That one is larger," he noted, nodding toward an oddly shaped variant in one corner.

"An experiment," explained Dutsa. "To carry heavier loads. I've seen men dragging things about behind them on pallets and decided a wheel would make it easier." He placed himself between the two shafts, facing away from the wheel. "This could be done by a pair of men," he said, and began pulling the device about. "I think I'll add a leather harness, too. Why, it might even work to carry goods over the hills instead of using pack baskets."

Hidlat audibly sighed. "A marvel." Then he suddenly broke into laughter. "I can imagine my wives being carried about so!"

Dutsa chuckled at the idea. "I don't think it would replace a litter. It would bounce too much." He gave Hidlat a looking over. "It would be a long way to carry one of my barrows home, wouldn't it?"

I was surprised. "You know where Hidlat's home is?"

"The news is all over the village. Can't hide something like that! And I got a good look at Kohari warriors years ago, anyway. I was one of those who raided that temple."

"Ah. Perhaps we fought each other sometime," spoke Hidlat. "I was not at the temple when it was burnt but I accompanied those who invaded the Mora lands soon after, seeking retaliation." He shook his head. "We were fools to attempt it. I barely escaped."

"Not me, sir," said Dutsa. "I never fought anyone again after that night and I'm glad of it." He gazed around his ramshackle workshop with obvious pride. "I'd rather make things than destroy them."

"Most of us would, my friend," Hidlat said. "Most of us would."

13. Families

THEY MARCHED AWAY the next morning, Gordie and Hidlat, Oorto, three of the warriors. The wounded man would stay on a time at the village. Gordie's last words were to Taki. "I trust you to keep my family safe until my return."

His family. He had included me in that. Yes, I did feel a part of Gordie's family. What part I could not say! Maybe I should ask Malee to call me Aunt Ranadi.

Hidlat — so he had been part of that Kohari army. What was it, eight years ago they had scaled the cliffs? I was not sure. Maybe more than that; it was before I came to live among the Mora. Oh, there had been talk of it at the temple but I was still very young. Even younger was I when the Mora burnt it to the ground while rescuing prisoners, initiating the war. I recalled flames and people rushing about and little more. I and my fellow dancers cowered in a corner of the compound, keeping well out of the way!

Some of my friends had fought in that war. Bafa had been something of a hero of the struggle. Poneiva himself had been a young warrior in the service of King Arierona. None of this had I told the Kohari nobleman.

I must ask Ulani to give me the epic of it sometime, though he did not compose it. Was it a work of his master, the Taona Isa? No matter; if Ulani wouldn't sing it I could surely persuade Toare to.

"Your father will be back soon," I assured Malee, though she had heard this more than once. Maybe I assured myself, too. "We can stay with Tala and Taki until then."

"And Eeto?" She looked up at me and then, shyly, at Hito's parents.

"Yes, Hito too," Tala said, as we ascended the wooden stairs to their house. "Once," she continued, apparently addressing me, "I would have been concerned about our child's future for, as with me, he would not be able to claim a Mora birthright."

"Despite being three of four parts of Mora blood," said Taki.

"Gordie has changed this. There is a place for us now."

"And for Hito," Taki said. "Yet it would be good if he could be accepted as Mora."

For that, the boy would have to be adopted into a Mora family, even as I was. I had learned enough of Mora customs and taboos to know all this now. Indeed, I could adopt Hito.

Or Malee, for that matter. It was something to consider. Not something to speak of. Not yet.

Taki sighed quite loudly. Almost a moan it was. "I must go do my duties," he announced.

"Meetings with various traders, mostly," Tala informed me as the big Mora ambled off. "If there is anything important to decide, he comes and discusses it with me." She looked fondly toward his disappearing bulk. "He has learned this is best."

"Gordie would never have asked he be named the Mora representative here, were it not for you," I said. Not that this was any news to her. The blustering but not not always sensible Taki and the shy, practical Tala made a good team. Most agreed on this.

The mention of Gordie turned Tala's thoughts in another direction. "Gordie misses Demba greatly," she said. "It can be seen, hide it as he will."

"Yes. It is so. I am glad I could help."

She gazed at me for a few seconds before speaking. "We all loved Demba. I think I resented you a little when you showed up here with Malee and her father."

"I can not replace Demba," I stated. Nor would I wish to.

"But you must be mother to her for many weeks to come, when you all go off to the Mora homeland."

"And where we will part." I did not expect to ever come back this way, did I?

"That may be hard on the girl," was all she had to say on that.

It would. "Maybe she would be better off staying with you."

"Maybe. But I think her uncle wants to take her with him."

49

"Oh, Oorto." I frowned. "He might choose to stay in the Mora lands too."

"I've heard he has a lover there," said Tala. "Things may be awkward between him and Pahe."

The two had been together when first I came to this land. Indeed, they had been the first humans Hito and I met as we came down from the mountains. "Maybe we need to find Pahe a lover," I said, "so he is not so *bitter*."

Tala laughed deeply at this though I did not think it quite so funny.

"Is Pa-ay coming?" asked Malee, turning her attention from the doll that must do until Hito woke from his nap.

"I do not know, little one," I told her. "You like Pahe, don't you?"

She nodded, her eye lids drooping sleepily. It was maybe time Malee had a nap too. "'E 'elps Daddy. Like you."

Tala nodded knowingly. "And for the same reason, I think. You both care about the man."

14. A Dream

NEARLY TWO WEEKS passed until Gordie returned. I was bored and spent too much time wandering the market, looking at things I would never buy. At Dutsa's shop, too, I loitered, and asked him for tales of his comrades who had come from the sea, of Bafa and Marareta and the others. Yes, Gordie too.

Two weeks — I recognized that it took time. Nearly half of that was spent traveling to his house and back, and then there were many affairs to which he must attend before leaving. Not the least of these would be getting his Kohari guests on their way home.

"Hidlat and Habaccan mentioned some vague idea of visiting at the Great Falls, posing as merchants," he told us his first night back in the trade village." Gordie did not sound very optimistic of that happening. As to what plans or agreements had come of their meetings, he said nothing.

I suspected there were none. Those Kohari nobles had come to scout, to learn, not to make alliances. Not yet.

Was Gordie doing anything different with this trip to visit the High King Poneiva? I would not expect anything immediate to come of it. In truth, I think it was as much an excuse to visit old friends as anything else.

A day to rest and prepare and then we would set out for the House of the High King, the ruler of all the Mora. It was the morning of that day when Malee proclaimed over breakfast, "I saw Mommy last night."

"A dream," murmured Tala.

"Most likely," agreed Oorto, watching the little one lick taro paste from her fingers. "So far as I know, as far as any shaman knows, no has ever spoken with the dead nor discovered where they go."

"I believe they are simply — gone," said Gordie, his voice barely audible. "Lost forever to us."

"Perhaps so, Brother Gordie," replied the shaman. He spoke our friend's name in the Diwarna fashion, with the stress on the second half. So had Demba ever said it. "But maybe nothing is ever truly gone. All things are part of infinite being, and time is meaningless when we step outside our worlds."

But we lived in this one, Gordie and I and most others. We had not the powers of those like Oorto. Or Malee —

Oorto continued. "It is possible Malee saw something. Her gifts might be akin to the power of prophecy, the ability to see all things at once."

"As the priestesses at A'auwa," I said. I knew Pana'a saw things to come but did not understand how.

He nodded. "And as they, she must be trained." His eyes lingered again on Gordie's daughter. "She is young to show any ability. If she dreamed, it may have been without meaning."

"Or it might not," sighed Gordie. "I know she will have powers akin to yours, Oorto. Or to the son of Marareta."

"Yes. Already I teach Maratoa."

Malee looked up at the mention of the boy's name. "I'm gonna marry 'im!" she proclaimed. Then she helped herself to more melon.

I think none of us knew what to say of that, and then our minds were turned to other things. Pahe came in to report on the preparations for the trip.

Gordie nodded in approval to his second's words, before turning to the rest of us. "Pahe will accompany us on our trip."

Pahe's eyes widened. He had not expected this. "Would I not do better to tend to your house, my lord?"

"Your aides are competent and Taki will be near." He turned to the big man. "I would ask you to keep an eye on things." A slight smile. "At least from time to time."

"Certainly, Lord Gordie." The Mora noble glanced at his wife, to make certain she approved.

"And you, Pahe, will be more useful at my side," Gordie went on. "I do have enemies."

Pahe thought on this for a moment, before asking, "How many men?"

"The six who came here with us. That should do. We need no servants." His eyes went to Malee. "I think Ranadi can take care of my daughter."

"And Oorto," I added.

"Yes, and Oorto." Gordie's tone grew quite grave, though his face remained expressionless. "I know there are dangers in making this journey, not only for me, and not only for you, my friends. If anything happened to me, things would be upset in the north for some time. Trade would suffer. Not forever, I know. Even the most loyal of followers must move on after a while."

"Not I," vowed Pahe. "I would never rest until you were avenged."

"It is to be hoped that is unnecessary," spoke Gordie, smiling at last. "Yet whatever the outcome, this is a trip I feel I must make, and not only for myself."

15. To the Hills

"It has been years since I last crossed the hills, when Demba and I attended the marriage of Amirea and Aranu. I was no more than a successful trader then, who walked into the Mora homeland without an entourage." Gordie was much more than that now.

There were eleven of us, and we had attached ourselves to a band of traders heading south. Several carried pots from the workshop of Amlee and Tala; there was a great demand for them among the Mora. Indeed, I suspect some of our warriors had slipped trade goods into their own packs, hoping to make a little profit from this trip.

For the most part, they were curious about the Mora lands. Oh, some had dwelt there; I believe a couple had even been born there. And one was a young Mora man who had left his home for one reason or another. That was not the sort of thing one asked about.

Pahe walked ahead of us. Things had indeed been awkward between him and Oorto. I did not think they had exchanged one word so far. Perhaps they had nothing to say to each other.

We trudged on, the path between pass and trade village well marked. More and more traders walked it with each season — and each of those traders meant more wealth for Gordie. Anything that came out of the Gurang valley came with his approval these days.

Savanna spread on either side, rolling grassland. "Further that way," said Gordie, gesturing to our right, to the west, "this prairie gradually merges with marsh. Beyond that lie the coastal mangrove forests. Heho once showed me some of the paths there, the paths he used in his days as a courier."

I looked westward. "What message would he carry into a wasteland?" I wondered. Surely no one lived there other than wandering tribes of Diwarna.

"There is a secret gap in the cliffs," was the explanation. "Now we have another pass, further east."

I knew of this. It had figured in the tale of Teme and Bafa. "It is not so easy to use, I understand."

"No, it is steeper and narrower. I have set some of my men there anyway, to claim the way." Gordie chuckled. "To the displeasure of Mahutunoa."

"I hear he and Naire argue as to which of their kingdoms the other end opens into."

"It matters little, now. Maybe in time. If we had wished to go directly to Lake A'auwa and the House of Arierona, it would be a quicker way. You will want to visit your friends there, won't you?"

I nodded. Of course I would. "I would like to see the famed lake," he said. "Only Dutsa and I chose not to go there when first we came to your land."

"You had a good reason," I told him. His love for Demba had taken him back to the swamps of the Gurang.

"The best of reasons," he agreed. The subject was not revisited as we walked on toward the distant line of hills. Those rose steep on this side, often standing as cliffs. Good ways through, easy of passage, were few, though one could probably climb over them almost anywhere, had one a mind. To our east, they grew ever higher, merging eventually, I was told, with the far mountains. Further west, they curved southward to become the sea-facing cliffs of the Mora homeland, their greatest defense against invasion.

Malee walked sometimes with us on her short legs, and sometimes one or another would carry her. There was no hurry; we stuck to the pace of the laden traders, even though it added a day to our journey.

On the second day, a misty rain swept in on the mid-afternoon breeze. "The first sign of the rainy season," remarked one of the traders. "I'll be happy to be home before it starts storming every day."

"Ah, but with those like you snug in your huts there will be more profit for the rest of us," rejoined another, to laughter all around.

The nights were still clear, the stars thick above us. No more did I spy Lugan in the evening sky, gone to wherever she slept when she hid herself from mortals. I had not thought on such things in a long time.

Rehe, the Mora called the evening star, and Rehe too was a goddess. Was she the same as Lugan, only named differently? That was beyond my knowledge. Maybe it is beyond all men's knowledge. I would learn more of Rehe when I returned home, I decided.

Home. Among the Mora, that was home, and maybe on the shores of A'auwa was where I would choose to dwell. Maybe even with Hito. All that seemed as far away as the stars right then.

Malee slept. All slept, save a sentry and Gordie and I. The young man from beyond the sea — from another world — sat beside me. Nothing was said for some time, both of us staring into the sky.

Then Gordie looked upon his sleeping daughter. "Malee loves you," he said.

"And I love Malee," seemed the proper reply.

"We would both wish you might stay with us," Gordie went on. He looked again at the stars, as if he might read his fate there. "Would you become my wife, Ranadi?"

I had always known when a man was interested in me. I say this as a fact. But I had not expected this from Gordie. "You — you wish to marry me?" Had Gordie fallen in love with me? No, he couldn't have.

"If you will. I have surprised you, I know." He laughed. "I have surprised myself, I think."

"I love you, Gordie, but I had not thought to love you in that way." Yet, why not? I asked myself.

"And I admit I do not love you as I loved Demba. Perhaps I never could." Even by starlight, I could see the sorrow on his face.

"You need not answer me. Think on it, Ranadi, while we are among the Mora and then let me know if you will return home with me." With that, he rose and went to his sleeping place.

I sat a little longer, and once more turned my eyes upward, to the silent stars. I could not read my fate there, either.

Part II. Many Houses

16. Choosing a Way

WE STOOD IN the gap, gazing out across the Mora homeland. It did not look greatly different from the land we had just left, though the hills sloped more gently on this side.

"You must call me Rahiniti now we are among Mora." I giggled. "Lady Rahiniti, if you will."

Gordie smiled at my jesting but I am sure he recognized it was also good advice, serious advice. He did not know the ways of the Mora well. I could help there. "Then I should be Lord Gordie, should I not?" he asked.

I tilted my head at him, trying to look as thoughtful as I was able. "You should be King Gordie," I told him. "You could claim the title in your own realm and none would be able to say otherwise."

"Why not High King?" he asked. "There is no one higher than me in those lands."

"Poneiva would not like that one bit! He might challenge you to a duel." The thought of Gordie facing the large and skillful warrior who ruled over all the Mora made us both laugh.

"I could practice on Taki," he suggested, "but I think I'll stick to nothing more than lord as my title." Gordie thought on that a second or two before adding, "For now."

I had a general idea of the path we should now take. Oorto had a better one but both of us thought it well to defer to the traders who had walked these ways many times. "I'm angling off to Marihana, that direction," said one, pointing nearly due south. "My canoe is there."

"Ours too," spoke another, with a nod toward the woman who accompanied him. It seemed the most common route — only one man was headed more east of south, closer to the coast. But that was the way Gordie remembered from his visit.

"That path will take us to the House of Revaru, won't it?" he asked. "We could visit there first."

"It would be out of the way," Oorto felt. "Even though we aren't taking to the water, Marihana's not a bad place to cross River Teiri."

"I think Poneiva would expect us to come to him first," I added.

Gordie grinned. "The High King may expect what he wishes. We go to Revaru."

It was Pahe who whispered to me later, "My master did not want to cut across so much of Mahutunoa's realm. Better to take this road and be away from his kingdom." That did make sense. It was simpler to avoid the king at this point — an invitation to his house before speaking with Poneiva would be awkward.

And this way was pleasant, I found. We soon passed into the kingdom of Anana, where there were more villages, more fields and orchards than further east. With my tattoos proclaiming me a high noble, I received only deference in those villages and none asked questions. I was again Lady Rahiniti, and Gordie and his men were assumed to be my entourage.

I do not think Gordie had realized quite how high my position was among the Mora. Oh yes, I have truthfully told you I had neither wealth nor a home. That mattered little at the moment.

As we journeyed, I could not help think on Gordie's proposal. I loved the man as a friend, maybe even as a brother, and I loved his Malee. Did I love him as one I would wed? I thought not, not truly, but maybe I should not care. Being the lady of the House of Gordie could be a good life, even if it did stand far from all my friends!

Well, give an answer before he left, Gordie said. I would have weeks. And I thought I would wish to speak to Hito before making a decision, and Teme too. Gordie said he wished to visit A'auwa and the House of Arierona so I would have the opportunity.

"If you continue on this path," our trader companion told us, "you will end up at Lake Aedina and the House of Va'aru. You should turn aside soon if you go to visit Revaru."

"We shall still have to cross Teiri somewhere," Oorto pointed out.

"There are canoes," I said, as if it were of no importance. "If Revaru knows we are coming he will provide." The young king certainly would know. Poneiva probably knew by now also.

Revaru was a good boy. He would welcome us. A boy, yes — a couple years younger than me, I would guess. I am not completely certain of my own age; I could not say exactly how old I was when I was taken to the temple of Mihasa nor how many years I dwelt there. But certainly older than Revaru, or Teme and Toare, for that matter. They were all about the same age and both young men had pursued Teme until she chose Bafa as her husband.

"That is the proper road," we were told in one village, a good-sized one nestled among groves of bananas and papayas, and tall palms. "It will bring you to the river near the king's house." There was a local nobleman's house there where we might have expected a meal and beds but Gordie wished to move on.

"Revaru's house is nearly on the river as I remember," he said. I nodded although I had never visited and had no idea how close it lay to Teiri.

"It will be good to stop and rest a while," I offered.

"It will," agreed Oorto, "but not for too long."

I agreed. "I yearn to stand soon by A'auwa."

"It would be good to see Ruiru," he said.

Pahe reacted to this. "Ruiru? Lady Teme's bodyguard?" I

think it was the first time he had directly addressed the shaman since leaving the trade village.

"Now a priest of Wenatu," Oorto informed him. "He dwells at a shrine he built by A'auwa."

"And you two — ah, that is good, I think." He turned his head to our destination and said no more.

No more than an hour later we came to a village on the River Teiri, a handful of huts, a dock, and could spy a similar place on the far side. I was not surprised at all to see several canoes pulled up on the shore and their crews awaiting us.

17. Revaru

"We did not come by quite this way last time," said Gordie. "I know we crossed the river somewhere further up. Right Oorto?"

"So I remember," the shaman replied. "Not as far up as Marihana for there were still rebel forces roaming that area."

Oh, these two had traveled together then. I had known this, had I not? But I had not thought of it. That was Oorto's first visit to Mora lands. "It doesn't matter, does it?" I asked them.

"Not in the least," replied Gordie. He grinned at Oorto. "But I would expect a Diwarna tracker to remember his way."

"And you, my brother, can find your way through our swamps as well as any Diwarna." The craft bumped against the shore and the dark shaman stepped out. I followed; Gordie, perhaps without thinking, attempted to assist. As if I can not get out of a canoe by myself!

His men were quitting the other canoes. Who was that in the water? Someone had decided to swim — ah, it was the young Mora warrior. He would know all rivers in the Mora homeland were safe, quite unlike those in the Gurang basin, where monster crocodiles lurked everywhere. Or so I have been told.

And there was the young king himself. "Welcome," he called. "Gordie! It is good to see you again. I, um, offer my sympathies." He glanced at an aide by his side, perhaps making sure he had worded that correctly. Revaru was noted for his courage but not much else. "And Oorto. Welcome, Friend!"

Then he spied me. "Lady Rahiniti?" In truth, we had rarely been in the same place at the same time, he busy being king here, I running the household of Temani'itu before he passed. We knew each other mostly by reputation, I think.

"Yes, my lord Revaru. I have accompanied Lord Gordie on his journey here." Best get all that straight right away.

"And I greet you, Lord Revaru," spoke Gordie. 'Lord' was

proper for any ruling noble, even the high king. "We ask the hospitality of your house. I remember my stay here fondly."

Gordie was good at that sort of thing. He could sell crocodile hides to a Diwarna. It was probably best that he was the one to request hospitality, demonstrating that he was on an equal footing with me, a high noble.

"Of course! I would love to have you stay as long as you wish." The young fellow eyed me. "The Lady Rahiniti especially." There was no mistaking his interest. Mora are very forward about such things, in general, and Revaru was brasher than most.

And Teme's first love. They had fought constantly, she told me. I chose to move a little closer to Gordie, to suggest that we might be a couple. Not that I had any fear of this boy, you understand, just to make things simpler.

The way to his house was short; one could spy it from the riverside. It rose high, one of the largest of any king. Perhaps only that of the high king was higher, but I admit I have not seen all of them. For that matter, it was the first time to see this one! We passed among newly-planted fields as we went, ready for the coming rains. It was rich land here near the river, and rich was the kingdom of Revaru.

"There is one awaiting you," announced the king. "Poneiva sent him when he heard you were coming this way. One such as you," he said, addressing Gordie, "who came from the sea."

"Bobbie Beck?" Gordie hazarded. "Or Beka you call him, right?" I had known at once that Revaru meant Beka, Poneiva's adopted brother. I suppose Gordie was too far away, too caught up in his own affairs, to keep track of all that went on here.

"So it is," came the king's amiable reply. "He barely arrived before you."

"Is Palala with him, my lord?" I asked.

Revaru laughed heartily. "His parrot remained behind. But I have one of my own now!"

I whispered to Gordie, "He practically worships Poneiva and Beka. I am not surprised that he would imitate either of them."

He nodded. "That is good to know."

Beka lounged on the veranda, which ran all the way around the House of Revaru. He came down at once and gravely embraced his friend, saying something in their own language.

"None of that," said Gordie, in near-perfect Mora. I had hardly noted that he had shifted to the language when we spoke with Revaru, so natural had it seemed. "That world is gone."

Beka nodded and turned his attention to me. "Welcome back, Rahiniti. Teme has missed you."

"I have missed her, and the House of Arierona," I replied. "Is she there?"

"Yes. Bafa keeps her captive, I think!" He laughed at his own jest.

"I hope to see that house," spoke Gordie, "after visiting your brother. But first, I shall enjoy the hospitality of Lord Revaru."

"We wondered why you came this way," said Beka as we mounted the wide stairs.

"To avoid Mahutunoa, mostly," came Gordie's frank reply. "And I had good memories of this house."

Revaru swelled a bit with the praise of his home — and he was a quite big boy already. "You did not think Mahutunoa would do you harm, did you?" he asked. "That is not his way."

"No, though assassins have attacked me in my own home. Mora assassins." He let that sink in. "Someone in this land would like to see me gone. That is one reason I have come." He turned around to look at Pahe and his warriors. "Where might my men find food and shelter?" he asked. That was wise, for commoners — much less foreigners — would not eat with Mora nobles in this house. In some houses, maybe, but Revaru tended to go with the old traditions. Mostly, I think, because it was easier not to change things.

An aide took charge of Gordie's retainers with the king needing not utter a word. Revaru watched them go without much interest and then gazed at the mid-afternoon sun. "Is it too early to feast?"

"Never too early," spoke Beka. "At least for a little feast before the main one."

18. Speaking Afar

I HAD NOT seen it before but Teme had told me of Oorto's trances. He sat on the mat-covered floor of the dark veranda, his thoughts in some other world, while Gordie watched nearby. Gordie had known Oorto long enough to have some understanding of his powers, probably more than anyone else on this side of the mountains save Marareta.

And there was Malee sitting quietly just beyond her father, her bright eyes fixed on her uncle. It was she I had come seeking. I sank down beside the girl.

Barely perceptible, there was a relaxing of the Diwarna's body. He turned his head to look at us, almost as if puzzled by our presence. "Was that your great wizard?" asked Gordie.

The shaman nodded. "Yes, Hurasu. It is mostly he to whom I speak from afar. Sometimes others who dwell further away."

"In other worlds?" I asked. I did not really understand any of it but I had heard such an idea mentioned.

Oorto seemed fully returned to us now. "Had it the proper gifts, one should be able to speak with any thinking creature anywhere in infinite existence. In practice, we rarely connect with anyone not in our own world. Our own universe." He gazed up at the stars, playing hide and seek behind thin clouds. "I suppose there might be minds out there someplace, among the heavens, but have never heard of anyone communicating with them."

Gordie looked up too. "Perhaps we are alone in all that vastness."

"Perhaps," agreed the shaman. "Or maybe it is just too far. Any world I might send myself into is a variant of this one." He smiled and reached out an arm. "Close enough I can touch it."

"I would think that might lead to some paradoxes." Gordie sounded at once thoughtful and unsure.

"It might." Oorto shrugged. "Mostly it is a matter of endless worlds in which one might become lost. That is why a wise shaman does not venture far." His eyes turned to Malee. "The Lord of Visions sensed my niece. I think she was trying to join us."

"That sounds dangerous," I whispered.

"It is," agreed Oorto. "The more reason I should begin training her, as I am Maratoa."

"Then we must go to the House of Marareta," said Gordie.

I understood, of a sudden. This was why the lord of the north had come to the Mora. He intended his daughter to study here, learn to use her gifts safely. Malee might not be returning home with him.

"As you always intended, I think," I said.

Only a hint of the pain he felt was evident in Gordie's voice. "I knew it might be so."

Not for always, of course. He was not abandoning the girl. If I accepted his proposal of marriage, I would have a reason to remain with Malee, to care for her, whether in Marareta's house or some other, until it was time to go home. I must decide. My heart and head hurt from thinking of it.

Do not panic, I told myself. Let come what comes. There is time. I willed myself to relax, as I might have before I went out to dance for the crowds at the temple. And here, no one would beat me if I misstepped!

"Our host is about to sit down to feast," came the voice of Beka, as his tall figure emerged from the gloom. "It would be a shame if the guests of honor were not there." His tone moved from playful to serious. "And an insult."

Gordie rose. "Then let us go sit down with Revaru," he said. "Lead on."

"You present a protocol problem," Beka was saying as we entered the wide entryway. "No one is sure whether to treat you as a king or a nobleman." He turned his head to glance at us. "Rahiniti is a high noble, so her place at Revaru's left hand is assured."

"As is yours," I observed. Both of us *ari noe*, high nobles, by adoption. "He is still without a wife, is he not?"

"Yes. I don't think he has quite gotten over Teme marrying another." We entered Revaru's spacious central chamber. There were not really that many gathered at the mats spread on the bamboo floor. But more than enough food for twice their number!

A server showed Gordie to the highest place, at Revaru's right. I would have expected this; whatever his rank, he was the honored guest at this meal. Beka took a place just below him. Of course, I went to the king's left. Oorto? He had taken Malee away to her sleeping chamber and was unlikely to reappear.

"I want to know all about your home, Lord Gordie," spoke the young king, between mouthfuls of millet cakes and fried fish. "I would like to see the Gurang someday!"

"It is only water," replied Gordie.

I had to break in. "The widest river you will ever see, my lord. And with enormous man-eating crocodiles!" I knew what this boy wanted to hear.

"It's been many years since I and my crew-mates paddled up that river," added in Beka. "I've sailed past its mouth since." He nodded rather respectfully to me. "With your late father, Lady Rahiniti." He had loved the old sailor as much as I.

"Once when we went to burn that Kohari temple," said Gordie. He smiled at me. "And frighten all the little dancing girls."

I sniffed. "Not me. I was ready to go out and fight!" Which was a total lie. I cowered with the rest.

But Revaru was ready to believe it. "I have heard the songs of your courage, my lady. To cross the great mountains! That, too, I would like to do." He sighed. "But I must stay home and rule."

"Someone must," commiserated Beka.

"Maybe if we have another war I can get out and do something. It was good to fight beside you and your brother!" The king's eyes went to a man standing at the far side of the chamber, beside one of his aides. "I shall be right back," he said, rising. "Keep feasting!"

For a moment he listened to the newcomer's words, nodding, before he returned to his place. "It seems, Lord Gordie, a messenger from your home awaits you at the House of the High King," announced Revaru.

19. The Messenger

IT IS NOT so far from the House of Revaru to that of Poneiva. I
would not know how to measure such things but, of all the kings, I
think his home lies closest to the House of the High King.

And the way is easy. A broad road leads south and west, at
first running beside the Teiri, then turning away. Tall sapa trees
grew on either side, and fields extended away to our left. This was
prosperous country — little remained that marked the destruction
of the civil war a few years earlier. I was glad of peace, even if
Revaru was not!

Beka and his two attendants joined our party in this short
journey. We hurried not; neither my legs nor Malee's are made for
that, and there were pleasant places to lodge overnight. Inside, for
the rain was becoming more persistent.

No, we hurried not but we did go directly and dawdled
nowhere. A messenger awaited Gordie and that was a cause for
concern. But surely, were it important, Poneiva would have sent
him on to Revaru's house. Beka knew nothing, for the man had
arrived after he departed his brother's house.

We learned even as we approached that house, for one came to
meet us — Poneiva's chief steward himself. "Greetings, Heho,"
called out Gordie. "I heard you served here now."

The former courier embraced him. "Only because my wife
thinks I should be kept busy," he replied. "I greet you, Lady
Rahiniti," he spoke, turning to me. "And Pahe!" He switched
without a blink from Mora to the pidgin. "I never expected you to
leave the Gurang."

"Nor would he if I had not insisted," said Gordie. We walked
toward the high house. It towered above the trees about it, for all
this had been rebuilt and replanted since the rebels burnt it. "How
is your wife?"

"Ma'are is well. I see not enough of her — the High King is

forever sending her off as his representative to one noble or another."

"And you watch the children?" I asked.

"When I can! That I would much rather do than scold the king's servants." He turned then, his face serious, to Gordie. "Poneiva couldn't come out to meet you. He is too busy also! You may be sure he will feast you later and talk following that. But there is another matter."

Beka took an interest. "The messenger?"

Heho nodded. "He arrived badly wounded. And the man refuses to speak with any but you, Lord Gordie."

"Then let us go to him." We stood at the steps of Poneiva's front porch now. Women and men bustled in and out the house, on whatever errands they had. Heho must have scolded them well. "Stay with my family, Pahe." With those words, he followed Heho into the house, Beka and Oorto with them.

"Family," said Pahe, flatly. "Are you to be such, Ranadi?"

I had to be honest. "I do not know. Let's get Malee inside, and your men quartered and fed." I knew this house fairly well and could handle that.

"It would not be a bad thing. Not for Malee and not for Lord Gordie," was Pahe's opinion. But what about for me?

No time to think on that. I had other tasks. I showed the men to the buffet laid out — as ever — on a side porch and left them to the filling of their stomachs. Heho would put them somewhere later. Pahe and I lingered there too, for Malee was hungry and then napped in the warm afternoon, listening to the rain drip from the roof edges. I may have dozed myself.

Pahe was getting up. Ah, Gordie walked purposefully toward us, across the mat-strewn floor. Heho had come out of the house with him, but now was busy giving orders to servants.

"It seems," said Gordie, with no preliminaries, "that one of our men disappeared. Sukat was the name. It might be meaningless but it is also possible that he is a traitor and has gone to the Kohari."

Pahe scowled. Yes, he did that frequently but this was a particularly fierce scowl. "I know the man. He hates the Mora and did not hide his anger over you going to them."

Gordie nodded at this information. "The fact our messenger was attacked is not a good sign. I am of a mind to return home at once." He stood and gazed out over the High King's gardens for a few seconds. "I shall speak with Poneiva first. And we must send messages to my house."

"Shall I return?" asked Pahe.

"No. I want you at my side." He looked at the empty bowls strewn beside our mat. "I want some food too. Over there?" He started in the proper direction but a servant came hurrying up to him.

"My lord, your men, ah, refuse to go with me to the lodging we have prepared. They claim you must give the order."

"They are well trained," stated Pahe.

"And they stay with me," said Gordie, "whether I sleep in their quarters or they in mine."

"I know there are appropriate rooms," I told the man. "I shall come and pick them." Then I could not resist adding, "Lord Gordie must be treated as any other visiting king!"

20. Poneiva

"It is good that the man is recovering," felt the High King of the Mora, Poneiva. "We were amazed that he made it to our house so wounded."

"Attacked somewhere between here and the hills, I understand," said Beka. Only Poneiva and Beka, and their wives, E'eva and Miruhata, sat down to that evening meal with Gordie and Oorto and me. Pahe remained with Malee; Gordie would trust no other with that duty. Oh, Palala was there too, on his perch. The green and gold parrot must have been sleepy for there was none of his usual invective.

"Yes. I have sent two messengers, a couple hours apart, to bear your words to Taki, Lord Gordie. He will send word on to your people."

"We must prepare for a Kohari fleet to come up the Gurang," said Gordie. "I shall return swiftly."

Poneiva and Beka exchanged a look. What had those two in mind?

"We see this," spoke the High King, "as an excellent opportunity to trap and destroy that fleet."

"If you don't mind us helping you out, of course," added Beka, helping himself to another chunk of succulent pork. Miruhata shot him a disapproving look.

"We shall be helping each other, I would say." Gordie replied, with the slightest of smiles. "That sort of thing is why I came here, is it not?"

The brothers could only nod agreement to that.

Oorto brought up something I had wondered myself. "Who would have attacked the messenger? No Kohari wander in this land."

"None that we know of," Poneiva said. It seemed a rather enigmatic answer to me!

Gordie said, "There must have been a Mora hand in that, someone who saw an opportunity to hurt me."

The High King nodded soberly. "There are those who mistrust you. Who fear you."

"They do," agreed Beka. "You've come a long way, Gordie, from a green boy on his first voyage to a self-made king."

Gordie smiled at that. "I'm not ready to claim that title yet. Maybe I should just go with 'Cap'n,' as Bamiree calls me.

"Bamiree?"

"Henry Wise. That is his name among the Diwarna."

"Oh. I remember Henry. The man could throw a punch. Maybe as good a one as Marareta."

The conversation then meandered off into reminiscences of their first days in this world and the prowess of Marareta in something they called 'boxing.' "Will we leave at once?" I asked after a time.

"I will leave," answered Gordie. "I want you and Malee to remain safely here." He frowned in thought. "Maybe Pahe should stay with you."

Oorto disagreed. "You will need him at your side. I can take care of Ranadi and your daughter." He regarded me thoughtfully. "Perhaps we should go on to the House of Marareta and wait there."

"Yes," Gordie agreed. "And I will go north at once."

"Not at once," said Poneiva. "You must remain tomorrow so we may make our plans for war. And I must feast you, for appearance sake. Then you may slip out and be on your way home. With a few of my warriors along, as a precaution."

"And you and Malee must come visit with us," E'eva told me. Miruhata nodded her agreement to this. I would rather have been with the men when they planned their strategies. Teme would have insisted on this — and her brother, the High King, might well have permitted it. For me, there was no chance. Maybe someday my wisdom would be sought!

For now, I sought my bed. Tomorrow would come and could be dealt with then. I had personally made certain Heho and his staff found us suitable rooms, close together, in the southern wing of this great house. Pahe and Gordie's chamber adjoined that of Malee and me, with a connecting way.

Ready was I to slumber, the girl already abed, when I heard Pahe enter. His voice sounded urgent. Why should I not know what was going on? Gordie but glanced at me as I entered his room.

"Ri'i, it was," Pahe was saying. This was the young Mora warrior among Gordie's entourage. "He met a man secretly in the gardens and then both slipped away, as if they did not wish to be seen."

"So, a spy, perhaps," said Gordie. "I included him for his knowledge of Mora ways. Perhaps it was not a wise choice."

"We did know little of him," Pahe observed.

"Does he know we are leaving?"

"No, my lord. I have told no one."

"Hmm. I think we will not confront the man for now, but only watch him. Questioning him might be of no avail, anyway." He gave a firm nod of his head, having made a decision. "I shall let the High King know we suspect a spy on the morrow."

Or maybe the boy just has a lover, I thought, or spoke with a friend. I would not speak these thoughts but only bade the men a good night.

21. Departures

THE NEXT MORNING, I did visit with Miruhata and E'eva and their children. All these were younger than Malee and she became bored with them, sitting and watching the adults instead, her expression grave. How like to Gordie she was when she did so!

Then we both napped. Malee for that is what five year old girls do, and I because I expected to feast late into the night. Our room lay in the interior of the House of the High King, and was a bit close despite the loosely-woven mat walls. But both I and Gordie felt it safer to remain there, with at least two of his men nearby.

Neither of them Ri'i, you may be sure.

I had not the heart to tell Malee that her father was leaving, would hurry away in the night with his men. Even Pahe, whom the girl loved. And who loved the girl, I had come to realize. It was in his care she would be left while Gordie and I attended the feast of Poneiva — he the guest of honor, I an honored guest.

The feast? Like many another I had attended in great Mora houses. The guests were all noble, men and women, though Poneiva readily shared meals with commoners on other occasions. Again, Gordie was accorded the place of honor, at the High King's right hand. I, however, could not expect quite so high a seat and was a few places down on the left. Ha, were I married to the man, I would be up further!

And his own status would be clarified, some, as husband to a high noble. That of his children, too. We would surely have children. Stop dwelling on all that, I told myself. I would not see Gordie again for weeks, maybe months.

So I gave my attention to the roast fowl and the pork, to the fish brought fresh from the Teiri or Poeneiva's own ponds, to the yams and taro, the many varieties of fruit. All to be washed down with plenty of good millet beer. Or the Mora claimed it was good; I had never developed that much of a taste for it and preferred palm wine. Too rarely served, that was!

Later, Gordie kissed his sleepy daughter goodbye, saying he would be back soon, that Ranadi and her Uncle Oorto would take good care of her. Out in the torch-lit dark, Pahe would be gathering his troop, men who had no idea they would be marching away this night.

And with them, Gordie. When he was gone I tried to sleep. I suppose I did, but was restless. Wander, I would have, had I not the duty to watch Malee, wander about this house, the gardens, the porches where others who did not sleep would gather, to eat and drink, to listen to songs and tales. Well, I would wander in the morning, wander far to the House of Marareta.

It was Oorto who awakened me, before the dawn. "A canoe awaits us at the river," he told me, "and breakfast here." His arms were full of bowls of fruit and cold meat.

"We will go down Teiri then," I said. Obviously; I might not have said that were I more awake. "Past the House of Temani'itu. The House of Pua, now, I should say." I looked up at the shaman. Once he had been lover to Pua's adopted son, the bard Ulani. They had been very young then — it was before I came to this land. Before Ulani himself had come to this land, for the two had met in the trade village beyond the hills.

"Yes," he said, and took a seat on the mat opposite me. "No need to stop." He glanced toward the still-sleeping Malee. "Poneiva has lent us a couple of his men, both as paddlers and guardians."

I added up the days of the journey in my head. Three, if we did not dawdle. The river was the quickest way, and the easiest way. All downstream! There were many places we could stop and rest, and, yes, the House of Pua was one of those, if we had wished.

Best I hurry and get going, I decided, or it might stretch to an extra night. We had little to gather together, all my belongings and those of Malee — save her doll — fitted into one basket and we were ready. The House of the High King lies at some distance from the river, and hours we walked through the mists of morning. A

78

remnant of those mists still stood over Teiri when we stroked out onto the river. Only Beka had bid us a farewell.

"I might stop by Marareta's house on my way to the coast," he told us. "I'll be helping to prepare the fleet, and will sail with it." Undoubtedly, messengers were already headed there, to report to Naio, who commanded below the Great Falls, where once Temani'itu had held sway.

The Teiri is wide and shallow and gentle, and many prosperous lands lie along it. We passed fields and orchards, villages and lone houses, and docks rising above the water. This was the heartland of the Mora realm, where Teiri and Teoma came together and then flowed on to the ocean. It was lovely to look upon but boring after a time.

I stroked a paddle with the others, in our one sizable canoe. How much I helped the three men, I know not! Malee was timid, for she had never traveled in a craft upon the water before and had always been warned to keep well away from the river by her home. With good reason, for great crocodiles lurked there. Here, there were none, only smallish ones whose diet was fish.

It was late afternoon when I spied the house where once I had lived happily, to our left. It lay close by the river. Perhaps I sighed at the sight.

"Toare is there," Oorto said, his voice almost a whisper. "His master, too." He meant Ulani.

I had traveled with Toare, once, up the Teoma to Lake A'auwa and the House of Arierona. Only a year ago, it was. It seemed so distant now. Teme had been with us on that journey, and Ruiru, her bodyguard. Then the girl had run off and had adventures while I remained. Not that I minded!

It would be good to see the boy. "Would you mind greatly if we stopped there?" I asked. I know, we had both intended to paddle by. So I changed my mind.

"There is no reason not to," the shaman replied. "Over there," he said to our two Mora, pointing toward the sandy bank where other canoes rested.

Years had I lived in that house, and a year had passed since leaving. I had not set foot in it since the funeral of Temani'itu, the event that sent me off wandering, to end up at A'auwa and, eventually, the House of Gordie. Pua would not mind if I visited her brother's grave mound.

A woman stood on the shore, a large woman, watching a child who waded and splashed in the shallow water. She squinted at us, the setting sun in her eyes. "Rahiniti?"

"I greet you, Lady Ma'ave," was the polite thing to say. So I said it.

22. Pua

I KNEW LADY Pua well, and liked her. Her daughter, not so much of either. But Ma'ave had helped Teme escape when she was held captive and that was to her credit. She called the little girl to her.

"Aeta, this is your cousin, the Lady Rahiniti." Her eyes turned to my companion. "You know the Taona Oorto." I had never heard that Mora honorific applied to him — nor any Diwarna — before.

I beckoned Malee to me. "Malee, greet the Lady Ma'ave." I had to speak this in the pidgin, as the girl knew little Mora. She did so, quite gravely and politely; do not assume she had learned no manners in the House of Gordie! "Malee is the daughter of Lord Gordie," I explained.

"Ah." The Mora woman nodded. Perhaps word of us had traveled here. "I welcome you both." She peered at Malee. "This is my daughter, Aeta," she said.

Aeta, I knew, was a year younger than Malee, though they were of a size. No, of a height — Aeta was surely the heavier of the two. Her family tended to size. The girl was staring at Malee's doll. "Who is that?" she asked.

Malee understood enough to give an answer. "Tamba," she announced, holding the straw-filled figure up. Yes, as Hito named me, 'Companion' in the pidgin, when we traveled together.

Pahe had made that doll, carved a head from kuru wood, attached it to a soft leather body. Even the little bark-cloth kilt he made — and remade, for it was frequently torn or lost. I think maybe Tamba preferred to go naked.

"'Ere," said Malee, and handed her Tamba to Aeta. "Be good to 'er!" I was not sure Aeta understood her words. Noble Mora did grow up learning both their own language and the pidgin, but Aeta was very young. She certainly understood how to treat Tamba, and rocked the doll in her arms, smiling.

"You travel to the House of Marareta?" asked Ma'ave, as we strolled toward the house. Little had changed here, had it? The faces of the servants were familiar, most of them, and I remembered where each tree stood and even when some were planted.

"We do," I answered. "Oorto will remain with us there as Malee's guardian."

"Her uncle, is he not? It is hard to lose a sister. And a mother."

"And a greatly loved wife."

"Yes, that too." She glanced behind us to see if the shaman were listening, but his focus seemed to be on the two little girls. "I lost a spouse recently too — but on purpose!" Ma'ave snickered at that.

I had to smile despite myself. Yes, she had rid herself of her husband, divorced Iro, who had been mixed up in the wrong sort of politics with the wrong sort of people. All knew Ma'ave was ambitious and had married the man as much to advance those ambitions as aught else. "He was a fool," she continued, "and I was a fool to wed him. But he did give me Aeta."

Among the Mora, who inherit through the female line, Aeta would be an important woman some day. As was the woman walking beside me; most likely she would take possession of this house when Pua went to the gods. And both she and Aeta could be mother to a future High King.

But it had been prophesied that the son of Teme and Lord Bafa would be raised to the dais, prophesied by the Priestesses of the Moon at A'auwa. How closely was this woman related to Lady Teme? Fourth cousin, maybe? These Mora carried long genealogies about in their heads but I did not have the memory for it.

Nor for the great epic poems their bards could recite nor even the long messages couriers learned on one listen and repeated flawlessly. For such things, one must train from the time one is a child. I was learning only one thing when I was small and that was to dance.

Someone must have run ahead with news of us, for Lady Pua stood on her porch, ready to greet her visitors. She had grown more stout; this I could see. No longer was she the powerful counselor to the High King, the woman who had trekked across the Mora nation, carrying his word, advising kings and nobles. I doubted she left this house much, anymore, though Poneiva still valued her thoughts.

"Welcome back, Rahiniti," she spoke. "Know that this always remains your house. And Oorto. It is good to see you." Her eyes went to Aeta and Malee, in earnest discussion over something, though I am not sure they understood each other. "And welcome to all," she said, turning her gaze to the two warriors. "There is food on the rear porch."

I walked beside her as we went around the house on the covered veranda, rather than through it.

"My cousin Poneiva sent messengers that you were at his house. Has Gordie remained there?"

"He hurried home. There is to be war with the Kohari," I confided to her. If I could not tell Pua this, who could I tell? Oh, all right, perhaps it should have been told to no one. "The fleet is being prepared."

"So my husband will be away somewhere once again. Naio should retire as admiral and come live with me, don't you think? This is truly the House of Naio! Let Beka take charge at the Great Falls."

"You could always find a second husband to keep you company," I said. This was one Mora custom of which I greatly approved.

Pua laughed deeply. "Perhaps I should steal Toare from my daughter!"

I could not hide my shock. "Ah, you did not know they were lovers," she said.

"It is — surprising," was all I could say.

The woman shrugged. "Why? Oh, she is a handful of years older than him, but still a young woman. And they both had lost in love recently." Her next words came almost as a whisper. "He and Teme were lovers, were they not?"

"Yes, for a season in the House of Arierona."

A nod. "Ulani would not speak to me of it."

"He was elsewhere most of that time. He left poor Toare to shift for himself."

"Serving the High King. My son has become more interested in politics than in poetry." She sighed.

I knew something of this. Ulani had often confided in Teme and, of course, my best friend confided in me. I rarely confided in anyone.

We helped ourselves from the bowls and baskets, and settled down on mats, not all together but in little groups. Malee and Aeta remained close to Oorto, who brought them fruit. It was obvious that Malee had declared herself the leader of the pair.

The two warriors found themselves a spot further away from the nobles. I doubt Pua would have minded if they had sat down with us, but such habits are ingrained in the Mora people.

And I found myself telling a very long story to Pua and Ma'ave, from the time I had left this house. Some they knew, of course. Some they themselves had taken part in. "So you were Lord Bafa's lover?" asked Ma'ave. "While Toare was with Teme?"

I had to admit it was so. Did she know that once Toare had mooned after me, when he was still a boy? Well, some after that, too. It might be best not to mention it!

"Where is Toare, anyway?" I asked. Or Ulani, for that matter.

"Off working on a new epic, I think," said Ma'ave. Her brow furrowed. "Or is it an old one?"

"An old one," Pua answered. "Toare has been learning some of the ancient tales his mother knows."

Ma'ave shrugged. "Nobody wants to hear those."

"Our cousin Poneiva does," came a soft voice from behind us.

Ulani. Where was his apprentice? Oh, over helping himself to the food, filling a bowl — no, two bowls. Ulani seated himself to Pua's right. "The High King thinks it right that the old songs be preserved. And I agree."

"Poneiva grows ever more traditional," observed Lady Pua. "Responsibility has that effect."

"Or it is his nature. Or both," came Ulani's amiable reply. "Ah, thank you, Toare." He took the bowl the young man handed him; Toare himself took a place on the mat with us.

"Are you to stay long?" asked the older bard, as he picked through the fruit, seemingly with little interest.

I glanced at my hostess. "No, we should hurry on to the Taona Marareta's house."

Ulani also looked to Pua. "It is time Toare and I journeyed there as well, Mother. I think we shall accompany the Lady Rahiniti."

23. Canoes

"TOARE IS GRATEFUL to get away from here," Ulani confided to me the next morning. We walked down the long slope to the Teiri and our waiting canoes. "He can escape Ma'ave at last."

I thought on that. "Could you not have taken him away at any time?"

"Ah, he needed to be tormented at least a little before I rescued him. And my sister was enjoying herself." I took a quick sidelong look at the bard, wondering how serious he was. He kept a straight face.

"I did not know you had much love for the Lady Ma'ave," I replied.

"We have become friendlier. And I must keep my mother happy." We paused at the river bank. "Ride with me today," Ulani invited. "We'll let Toare take the other canoe. He has had enough of my company, too."

Why not? Oh, but with whom should Malee stay? She was in Oorto's arms at the moment. That would be all right and we could switch later, if the little one wished. "I am not as strong a paddler as your apprentice," I warned.

"I am in no great hurry," was his only response. So it was, Ulani and I in one smaller canoe, the rest in the craft in which we arrived. Was Ulani yet avoiding Oorto? They had parted on good terms, the last time they saw each other. That was at Teme's wedding, the year past, by A'auwa.

A season had I remained at the ancient House of Arierona, before that wedding, listless, not knowing what I wished, while Teme went adventuring. So it was I decided to go and see if I could find something, somewhere, as well, and had set out for the House of Gordie.

We drifted as much as we paddled, that day, and the other canoe must need adjust its speed to match us. Long, we gossiped, Ulani and I, of all the things that had occurred in the homeland of

the Mora while I was gone. And, too, I told him of my own journeys, and of Demba and Gordie. He had known Gordie well, once,
and his Diwarna wife also. Oorto's sister — of course he had known
her.

We heard Toare's voice raised often in song. That was a good
thing for all of us and especially, maybe, for Malee. Little would she
have understood but it was as good a way as any to learn Mora!
Not quite to the Teoma were we when we pulled to the shore, to
sleep at one of the encampments for travelers.

"It is not so far to the House of Marareta from here," said
Ulani, as we pulled our canoe up onto the sand. "We should be
there by afternoon tomorrow." He gave me a slightly abashed look.
"But you know this. I talk too much."

Yes, I had traveled this way before, after the funeral of
Temani'itu. Then we had camped further down Teiri, near where it
joined Teoma. Ulani was usually careful of his words, both as bard
and advisor, but his tongue had loosened today.

Rain traveled with us and we were happy to take shelter in the
open huts there. Many travelers shared them; a prosperous land
means much trade, and much of that trade passed through the
joining of Teoma and Teiri. We shared a cold meal, watching distant
lightning and the coming and going of the heavier showers.

Malee sleepily slumped against me as I sat, oblivious to
anything else. Ah, was Ulani going to converse with Oorto at last? I
saw him squat beside the shaman, sharing a moment of speech,
before the man came over to me.

"Oorto may not miss anything in the swamps and jungles, but
among men I have the better eye," he said, settling down at my side.
"We are being watched. Do you know why?"

I did, and decided Ulani should as well. I could think of no
man better to fill in on all that had happened with Gordie and
Poneiva, and even Hidlat. It took some time.

"I have been away from the House of the High King too

long," he said when I finished. That and no more. But he did go and speak to each member of our group, whispering warnings.

What might interest anyone about us? None of us were of much importance, really. I found a sleeping mat soon after, Malee again close by me.

Darkness lay all around me when I opened my eyes again, but I could see a shape darker than the night standing near us. Not Ulani, was it? I reached over without thinking about it to place a hand on Malee, reassure myself of her safety. The figure slipped away.

Nothing maybe. Some trader going to relieve himself in the night, or a late arrival at the encampment.

Or not. As we breakfasted at dawn, Ulani said, "We took turns watching through the night. A man approached you but then backed away."

"When you moved," added Toare. "I was on watch then. Why would he be interested in you?"

I knew at once. "Not me," I said.

Ulani understood. "Malee." Oorto nodded in agreement.

"How better to coerce Gordie than to take his daughter?" I asked.

"The man who was watching us — probably the one we saw in the night — took to the river early. It is time we do the same and finish our journey to Marareta's house." Ulani rose. "And we must make certain to guard the girl carefully when we reach there."

24. The House of Marareta

BY THE MIDDLE of morning we stroked into Teoma, and turned north, moving still with the flow. Teoma was a greater river than Teiri, deeper, swifter.

Toare shared his master's canoe today, and I rode with my own party. We made more haste; there was a sense of urgency. This did keep me from watching the shore so much as we paddled, where men and women and many children played and worked. Fruit trees lined the banks, citrus and mulberry and even the kuru Hito so hated. Bananas sprouted by every house, sometime towering over their roofs. The raucous crowing of roosters mingled with the songs of a multitude of wild birds. This land awed me, as it had when first I paddled by with Hito.

There, on the left. I recognized the little village that lay close by the House of Marareta. "That's where we are going to stay a while," I told Malee. "You and me and Oorto. We'll wait there for your father." She was used to Gordie's frequent trips to attend to business. It was best to act as though this were the same.

The girl fixed her eyes intently on the approaching shore. "Maratoa is 'ere," Malee said.

"So he is," said Oorto. "I do not think he feels you as you feel him, Malee."

"You'll teach 'im," she stated.

There was nothing I could add to any of that. "Let us go meet him," I said, and lifted the little one over onto the sandy beach. "The taona should know we are coming. Poneiva's messengers travel more swiftly than we."

"I saw more than one of them pass us on the river," spoke one of the guards who had accompanied us. Hohanae, I think it was, but it might have been the other one.

Up the pathway from river to house we went, past the orchards, past Marareta's fish pond. A small stream bubbled to our left. Citrons lined the way, hung with the ripening oblong fruit.

"Oh, you're early!" someone cried. "Father! They're here!" A large young woman — a girl, really — turned to greet us. "Welcome! Oh, Rahiniti! It's good to see you again."

"And good to see you, Tita. This is Malee," I said, presenting the girl. Tita called Marareta 'father' now? That was good, I thought, and the way Mora did things. Her true father was the late High King, Maitoa. Marareta had married Tita's mother, Panoha, who now bustled out of the house, servants in her wake.

"Ulani! And Toare — we were not expecting you. I am sorry your mother is not here."

"I know well she is in the south," replied Toare. "She must spend some time with her husband, after all."

With Hito. Yes, Toare's mother, the Lady Mehetu, was the one who wed the warrior-turned-priest. A better match than ever I would have been.

Would I still consider the idea of being a second wife to him? It hadn't been in my thoughts lately, what with Gordie's proposal, but I was not willing to dismiss it. Second wife only in order of marrying him, of course, and not subordinate to Mehetu in any way!

"Come along, come along," she said to us. "We have rooms ready, and food. Marareta is somewhere around here."

Up the steps to the House of Marareta we filed. It was not a large house, and it was very old, one of the oldest in the land. I had heard it was built in the days before the first High King, when Mora warred on Mora, and was placed on a low hill for defense. A stockade had once stood about it but that was long vanished. Such were against the laws of the Mora now.

Almost I followed the others into the house, but I glimpsed something as I was on the stairs. Toare was at my side so I touched his arm and nodded my head toward my discovery. Two sea-colored eyes peered at us from beneath the house.

Toare crouched down. "Maratoa," he said, "why don't you come out of hiding and come meet Malee?"

"I don't want to see her!" the boy declared. "She's —" He couldn't seem to come up with a word.

"Scary?" I suggested. I think maybe that was about right but this boy would not admit to it.

"She's not scary! She's just a girl! And I'm going to be a great warrior."

"Then come out and behave like one," Toare told him.

As young Maratoa could not let himself be other than a brave warrior, he reluctantly left his hiding place. A sturdy boy he was, but not large — about a year older than Malee. I had to ask, "Could you, um, *feel* Malee was here?"

He nodded slowly. I suspect that would scare any sensible six year old. "Well, she is just a girl," I assured him. "And Oorto will make her behave."

"I remember you," he said as we mounted the steps. That he also remembered my name I doubted.

"Of course you remember Rahiniti," Toare said. "Who could forget someone so wonderful?"

I could agree with that, even were it said in jest. "We are related in some way, I am sure." I had to laugh. Every Mora noble seemed to have a tangled web of relationships to every other Mora noble. "I am cousin to Tita, anyway."

"I suppose I am related to you too," said Toare. "Now, Panoha is my aunt so I am truly Tita's first cousin. So I could count you a cousin as well."

Yes, Toare's mother had been wife to Panoha's brother, the late Hareata. But I would just as soon he didn't call me cousin. Hmm, Ulani could also be seen as cousin to both of us — and none of us shared an actual drop of blood.

Someone had found Marareta and he now stood in his common room to welcome us. A little girl held his left hand, his

91

daughter Rahiri. Malee looked at her with no great interest, before turning about and setting eyes on Maratoa. Those eyes remained there; were I the boy, I might have run and hid again.

"Messengers have kept me informed of what has been going on," the taona was saying. "Some of it. We'll concern ourselves with none of that for now." His attention went to the two men Poneiva had sent with us. "You are to remain?"

"Yes, my lord," one responded. "Remain close, we were told."

"I'll show them their chambers, Husband," spoke Panoha. "And when you wish," she said to us, "there is food on the south porch." She gestured in that general direction.

I, for one, was glad to settle into a room first, and get Malee settled as well. We followed the lady of the house and her servants down a hallway. "We'll put you in your mother's room, Toare," she said over her shoulder. "Um, Rahiniti here." She nodded toward an entry to her right. "And Oorto the next room. You two, across the hall," she said to the warriors.

Ulani? He had not followed with the rest of us. He knew the house well and would find a place. I much suspected the poet was conversing with the taona at the moment, before his other guests demanded his attention.

Malee looked about our room. It was much like any other room in a Mora house, though smaller than some. "Are we going to live 'ere?" she asked.

I wasn't really sure. "For a while. Let's go get something to eat. Want to bring Tamba?"

She shook her head and grinned. It was a wicked grin for so little a girl. "She might scare Maratoa."

We met Toare in the hall and all headed for the porch and food. Ulani was indeed there huddled with Marareta. Best not to intrude.

So we filled ourselves with millet cakes and cold fowl and fresh, sweet fruits on the south porch of the House of Marareta, the porch that overlooked his orchards. Few words we spoke. It was good to be here again, to be at peace if only for a while. Soon, Malee fell asleep. I saw no reason not to do the same.

25. Children

"BEKA STOPPED, BEFORE the dawn, and then was away again," Marareta told me. It seemed I had arisen before any other of my traveling companions — save Oorto, who now watched over a sleeping Malee.

"On his way to war," I said. A bowl of little oranges rested in the taona's lap. I should go get something too. News first — I sat down at his side.

"They ready the fleet quickly, with men who are at hand. There will be no calling for warriors from the nine kingdoms." He smiled. "But young Revaru knew something was afoot and travels with Beka. Between them, they had more canoes full of men than I could count." He chuckled. "Mostly because it was too dark."

I would have liked to have seen that. Someone should have awakened me! "That would still not be a great host, would it?"

"No. Nor is one needed. The plan is to catch the Kohari fleet between that of the Mora and Gordie's." He raised his eyes from the globe he was peeling. "I hear his boats are quite effective."

"But he hasn't that many." Nor men, either.

"The Mora love to gamble," was his response. Very true! I had learned this in my time among them. "They gamble now that they can inflict a great defeat and drive Kohari raiders from the Gurang for good." His smile mocked his own words. "Or a year or two, anyway."

I think maybe the Taona Marareta did not completely approve. He may also have recognized that there was no better course. By the time I had filled bowls to take back to my room, he had gone.

"It is time we brought my two pupils together," said Oorto, after we had broken our fast.

"Malee should also be learning the Mora language," I told him. I knew she would probably be picking it up just from being in this house. "You teach Maratoa in the pidgin, do you not?" Oorto was more comfortable with that tongue.

"It is more practical," he said, "but I have also introduced him to the language spoken beyond the mountains. He should learn how to speak with those who dwell there."

Oh. "Then you can not always understand when you, ah, speak from afar?"

"So it is. That is another reason why we rarely seek out those in other worlds. We most likely would not be able to communicate. Although —" He glanced toward Malee, momentarily preoccupied with Tamba. "There are ways to share thoughts without speaking. It is dangerous."

"I thought all of it was dangerous!"

I spoke somewhat in jest but Oorto answered solemnly, "It is the dangers which we must first address. These children should learn as soon as possible how to block all those worlds out there." He swept an arm widely. "Madness awaits those who can not. Maratoa has learned some. The rest can come in time."

I whispered my next question. "Has he as much, um, ability as Malee?"

"It has not come out much yet. Many do not give any sign of having a gift until they are much older."

Girls were always quicker at things, weren't they? "Then it is Malee who most needs your attention now."

Oorto nodded. "I made a start during our travels." He turned to the little girl. "Malee, do you wish to learn more about the other worlds?"

"Un-uh, Uncle Oorto. Tamba and me want to explore!"

"Good idea," I said. "Let's ignore the world until tomorrow. The other worlds too!"

She took my hand and down the hall we went. "Let's find Toare," the girl said. "'E sings!"

"So does Ulani, you know," I told her.

"'E's sad when 'e sees Uncle Oorto."

Maybe so. "I think he feels lonesome sometimes, Malee." Despite all his important friends, his acclaim as a bard.

Toare, it turned out, was exercising with the warriors. It was his custom when he stayed at the House of Marareta. He had done so during his time at King Arierona's house too, spent at least some mornings practicing the skills of war, the skills he had learned when younger, before choosing the life of a bard.

Ulani accepted his apprentice's quirk with amusement. "So great a talent should not waste his time on weapons," he said. "But he is a noble Mora. What can one do?"

"Age will take care of that," said Marareta. "Age and a wife, maybe."

"Not Ma'ave, I hope!" I had to add.

Rumors of this had reached the taona. "He would be an improvement over Iro."

There was no disagreement on that. Only the three of us dawdled on the porch, watching a knot of children playing below, at the edge of Marareta's gardens. Whence all of them came, I was not sure, but the taona apparently permitted this. I had met no Mora noble who would do so. Perhaps I had never realized before how different he was from the people among whom he now lived. We would never become truly Mora, either of us, would we?

Much less Gordie, who did not live among them. Was that why I had felt comfortable in his house?

Malee sat to one side, with little Rahiri, who was a year or more younger. She too had a doll, all of wood. I think she envied Malee her Tamba!

"I left a farm when I was young," said the taona, to no one in particular, "eager to get away. Now I like nothing better than to watch my crops ripen."

"My father was a farmer too," I murmured. But my mother was only his servant and concubine, and he did not mind selling me to those who trained dancers. The only good turn the man ever did me, that was.

Ulani laughed. "While I am the child of wanderers, my father a Mora trader, my mother of a Diwarna tribe. She wanders with them still so far as I know."

Laugh he might have, but we could both feel his sense of loss. "You found a new mother and she is a good woman," spoke Marareta.

"Yes, I am grateful to the Lady Pua," the bard said. "And my father did his best for me. He could have left me to fend for myself but instead saw to it I studied with Master Isa."

"And maybe someday, my friend," said the Taona Marareta, "you will have a little house by a river like Isa, where you may rest from wandering."

"Maybe someday, Taona, I shall want that."

26. Intruders

NONE SAT DOWN to official feasts in the House of Marareta. The taona was no great noble. An important man, yes, friend and advisor to kings, but he lived simply.

This is not to say we did not feast that night, now that we were all settled and rested. Panoha and Marareta were good hosts. Tita was old enough to sit with us at a meal, but no other children. That is the way in a noble Mora house. Malee we left in the care of Hepetea, wife to Marareta's personal attendant, Rika. Three children of their own they had, all younger than Malee.

I did not like leaving Malee, but both our warriors kept watch. Marareta, too, had set extra guards about his house. All should be well, I told myself.

After, Ulani and Toare took turns giving us the old epic they had been practicing, out on the south porch. The night had grown clear. Such there were, even when the rainy season was upon us. Lugan had not yet reappeared; I should look for her in the mornings maybe.

"I shall go take Malee to your sleeping chamber," Oorto whispered to me after a time. He slipped off without further word to any.

I need not hurry away, then. I could sit here with these, my friends, forgetting any cares until the morrow. Or maybe the next day!

"Father! Father!" A shrill cry, as young Maratoa burst onto the porch, quite naked. "Malee!"

Marareta rose. Perhaps all of us did — I was not paying attention to the others. "What of Malee?" he asked.

"She — I felt —" The boy attempted to untangle his tongue. "A bad man. He — hurt Oorto!"

Toare was the first to rush toward our sleeping chambers. He was young, and warrior-trained, so one must expect this. But I was not far behind. The others surely followed. I heard someone blow upon a conch horn, to raise an alarm.

The hall was empty. That was not surprising; no one had been ordered to stand sentinel. Toare burst into the room, through the mat that hung in its entry. "Oorto!" I followed him but could see naught in the dark.

One of our warriors pushed into the room, holding an oil lamp high. Now I could spy Oorto's form on the floor — and no one else. "Malee has been taken!" I cried out. "Did you see anything?"

The man appeared shocked by this news. "We escorted them to their chamber and then went to ours," he said. "Nothing did we hear."

"Through there," spoke Toare. The mat between this room and the next, Oorto's own sleeping chamber, had been rent. The young bard charged forward and the warrior followed him.

I crouched by Oorto. "Someone bring a light!" I called out. A moment later Ulani stood above, holding a torch in his hand. Dangerous to do so in a house but none of us cared at that moment! Blood was on the mats by the shaman's head. I felt his heart. He lived.

"Someone clouted him on the head," said Ulani. He let his fingers go to the wound. "I think he may not be too badly hurt." I knew one could not be certain with such injuries, but I hoped. Yes, and said at least one prayer to any gods that might be listening.

"That thick mop of hair may have saved him," the bard went on, attempting to keep his voice calm, matter of fact. But how could he not feel for one he had once loved? Still did, perhaps.

Marareta entered, and placed a lamp on the floor. "Best douse that torch," he said, before turning his attention to Oorto. "Water!" he called. "And cloth." Someone hurried away to fetch them; I paid no attention to that.

Part of me wished to stay and tend the stricken shaman; part wanted to follow Toare in his pursuit. Ah, what could I do for Oorto? I rose and pushed my way into the next room. Dark and empty. I looked out into the hall, at the group around the entry to my chamber. "Hohanae," I called, "bring a lamp!"

The warrior hurried to me, and we examined the room as he held his light high. All was intact save the torn wall through which I had entered. "The kidnappers must have gone out the entryway," said Hohanae. "That was bold. They could easily have been seen in the hall."

Not by you, I might have said, but held my tongue. If any were to blame, it must be Oorto and I for not being more cautious. "Come," I did say, and started down the hall, which opened onto the small northern porch. I could see torches moving about in the night. Where might a kidnapper run? The river? That seemed most likely but there were many ways to reach it.

Shouts arose somewhere to our right, distant. The lights moved that direction. What was happening? It would not do to go blundering into the night so we remained watching. I think maybe Hohanae, too, wished to act. He nervously shifted his weight from foot to foot, peering into the dark, and once or twice fingered the flint knife at his side.

Ah, the torches were moving toward us. Minutes we waited, minutes long as hours, until a figure became visible — Toare, with Malee safely in his arms. Men followed after him. Two dragged a body.

"One got away," reported Toare. "But we have Malee. That is what matters." He handed the girl into my embrace.

"Lord Toare himself slew the man," someone said. "He rushed upon him without fear!"

Hito had once described Toare to me as a reckless fighter. He disapproved of this but tonight I thoroughly *did* approve! We slowly proceeded up the hallway. "A few moments more and they would have been on the river, beyond our reach," he said.

"We must thank Maratoa," I said. "And I thank you, brave Toare."

Oorto was conscious by the time we reached our chamber. "I saw nothing," he admitted. "Someone struck me from behind as I entered." The shaman regarded our rescued Malee for some seconds before saying, "I understand Maratoa raised the alarm."

Marareta spoke, slowly, carefully. "My son tells me knew Malee was in trouble, somehow, and came to investigate." The taona gave no evidence that he found this in anyway strange. "He saw our intruders in the hall, escaping with the girl, and rushed to me."

"So," said Oorto, "already they have a bond."

27. Gifts

THE DEAD MAN was Mora; that was to be expected. Who might have sent him and his partner, none could say.

"Some faction that fears Gordie's power, one might conjecture," said Marareta. "Perhaps whoever planted the warrior Ri'i among his men."

Ulani's eyes widened, slightly, briefly, at the mention of that name. I know not whether any others noted this. It faded so quickly I was not altogether sure I had noted it myself.

And so all returned to normal in the House of Marareta, save that more warriors now stood guard. Oorto seemed none the worse for his bump on the head. Perhaps, indeed, his bush of straw-colored hair had saved him. It should surprise no one that talk turned to Malee and Maratoa at our meal that night. It was Panoha who asked the shaman of these things, but I wondered myself.

"I have explained all of this to Gordie in the past," he began. "And some you have heard, Mika." So did Oorto ever name Marareta, the name the Diwarna gave him when first he came to our world.

"But none other have," said Ulani. "I wondered about you often enough."

Oorto gathered his thoughts for a moment. "It is more a *sense* than anything else — the ability to see into the innumerable other worlds that exist. That is a gift with which one must be born. But one learns to use it, to perhaps find what is needed in those other realms or to use them to speak from afar."

"You actually enter those worlds, don't you?" asked Marareta.

"We do, in part. Only in part. Most sorcerers in this world inherited that gift from Hurasu. Perhaps all did. But perhaps, too, some of those who found their way here from other worlds also had the gift but knew it not. Hurasu told us it was almost impossible to use in the world he passed through on the way here. From that world came almost all our ancestors." He nodded toward Marareta. "From that world came your heroes from the sea."

"Then there could have been those who unknowingly had these abilities in our world."

"Yes. They could not use them. It is likely the heritage of such is in both you and Gordie, or your children would not be gifted." The shaman's gaze went from Marareta to Panoha and back. "Your daughter Rahiri might carry that heritage, though she seems to have no abilities."

Panoha pondered the puzzle of his words. "Then one of the parents must have this gift?" she asked.

"Not necessarily." Oorto, I think, now tried to explain something he did not understand entirely himself. "Or so Hurasu claims. But if both do, the children certainly will also."

Marareta laughed. "Mendelian inheritance! Bafa would know what that means but no other in this land."

"It is certain, anyway," continued the shaman, "that Gordie and Mika brought *something* in themselves. Maybe not exactly the same as what is in Pana'a or me or Hurasu himself, but something that led to Malee and Maratoa having their abilities."

"They will have a bond such as you had with Rahaita," spoke Marareta. "I envied you that bond, my friend."

"But you shared a far deeper bond, Mika."

I need not go into the tale of Rahaita and Marareta; there are epics that tell of their love and his loss. Moving, they are, but even more so was the tale as I had it from Teme, who was a part of it all, who had been there at the death of the taona's wife.

Would those two children love? Or would it only be a bond of friendship, of a sort of family? I am not one to look into the future; not even the Priestesses of the Sacred Isle, I think, would know the answer to that question.

Perhaps I should ask them whether *I* would love, when we stood again by A'auwa.

28. News

FIRST CAME A messenger, speeding up the river, telling his news at the houses of the great nobles. Weeks had it been since Beka had passed by, heading to war, and no news since — this we had expected, so long as the fleet of the Mora was at sea.

Victory. That was all, really, the man had to say. But enough, perhaps! As to whether Gordie, or any other man who had sailed, was yet alive, there was no word. The courier was given food and drink, he rested a few minutes, and then was again upon his way.

Malee and Maratoa had settled into their lessons with Oorto. Brief, they were, for both were very young and not long of attention. I think Maratoa was but a little afraid of Malee now!

Perhaps the rest of us grew bored, tired of waiting. I was eager to be on my way, though I knew not where, truly. Was my home in the south, at the House of Arierona? I could not say but it seemed the best destination for now. After that? There remained Gordie's offer.

Maybe I could decide, would know better my heart, when he returned here. Weeks more, that would surely be.

Ulani, too, seemed restless. Not his apprentice; Toare was happy to be again in the house where he grew up, practicing at being a warrior, making up new songs for us each day.

"My master wishes to be back in the High King's house, whispering advice in Poneiva's ear," he confided to me. "Messengers pass back and forth between the two every few days." The messengers I had noted, but thought they were Marareta's.

"You will soon leave him, will you not?" I asked. Every apprentice must some day part with his master.

"There is no hurry, and he is still introducing me in the houses of noblemen. So does a young bard become known." He flashed a smile. "And perhaps no apprentice every completely leaves his teacher. Ulani still sits with Master Isa from time to time."

I wondered if Ulani would take on another student when

Toare went his way. This boy had been his first apprentice; he was not really that much older than Toare.

More news came south over the following days, none of it in great detail. The fleet had returned to its harbor below the Great Falls, this we knew, and Naio yet lived and commanded. Of Gordie, no word at all.

"Revaru passed by earlier today," reported Marareta one evening. "My men saw his canoes. I think we may see Beka returning soon."

"He has duties with the fleet," observed Ulani. "In name, at least, he is Naio's second." There were chuckles. All knew that Lord Beka had little interest in commanding the canoes of the High King, nor in being successor to Naio.

"I would like to know how the great double canoes fared in battle," Marareta said. "They have never been tested."

These had been my adoptive father Temani'itu's last project before retiring, the fulfillment of a desire to build the largest canoes his people had ever known. It was Marareta who suggested the idea of the double canoe, though indirectly. The taona was not one to assert himself.

Two days later came Beka. Oh, we knew he would stop, for messengers had gone before him. In many canoes he and his men paddled up Teoma, but most paddled on. Only one craft pulled in at the little village by the House of Marareta, with but five men.

Having nothing better to occupy my time, I had spent the morning waiting for them. I and Ulani — Tita stayed a little while but became bored, splashing for a time in the water and then going home. The broad-shouldered Beka I could pick out easily enough from among those who pulled the canoe up onto the shore. My eyes went to the young warrior at his side, a rangy boy, with an open, homely face.

"Your brother, Mouiri," I whispered to Ulani. He was Pua's

youngest, making him a cousin, but I barely knew him. Nor had I set eyes on the boy since the funeral of Temani'itu.

The bard nodded. "Perhaps he passes on his way to visit our mother." He stepped forward to give them greeting, embracing both men.

I considered Mouiri. He was yet another young man who had pursued Teme — or had hoped to, for he was somewhat youthful. There was a political motivation, too, for the boy would have been a leading candidate for the dais of the High King had anything happened to Poneiva. Then I too greeted the pair.

As we followed the path to the House of Marareta, Beka clapped the young man on the back, saying, "Mouiri is of age now, ready to choose a warrior's life and serve somewhere."

"I have been learning the ways of a warrior at the House of Va'aru," explained Mouiri. I knew this custom of noble Mora well. So had Toare served at the House of Anana before choosing a different path.

"And it is I he will be serving," stated Beka.

That was certainly good politics. I wondered idly if Beka had come up with it himself. Then we were at the house and I thought no more of such things.

29. Beka

"GORDIE IS WELL and suffered no harm in our battle," Beka informed us. I had been eager to hear this but had not pressed.

"And Pahe?" I asked.

"Fought bravely and lived to tell of it," he replied.

"He was a hero of the battle," interjected Mouiri. This I could believe.

"Yes." Beka took another prodigious gulp from his bowl of beer. "We caught the Kohari exactly where we wished, at the mouth of the Gurang. Our fleet coming in from the ocean and Gordie's from the mangrove mazes."

"Room to maneuver," observed Marareta. "Mora canoes need that."

"That is so," Beka agreed. "We can sail circles around those Kohari boats but lose the advantage when we get close and fight hand to hand."

"Mora are *never* at a disadvantage fighting hand to hand," declared Mouiri. I think he had already had a little too much beer.

"I suppose not!" laughed Beka. "But when it comes to an exchange of arrows and spears, it might be better to be in a high-sided Kohari boat than a dugout canoe."

"There's plenty of cover in the large canoes," said Marareta.

"That's true. And they can run right over those Kohari boats, even the biggest ones. But they kind of got out of the way, most of the time."

"The double canoes can not turn so quickly," said Mouiri. He sounded almost sober when he said that.

"But we could rain down spears and arrows on them as we passed. Of course, they tried to run up the Gurang when we swooped in from the sea."

"And Lord Gordie's boats were waiting. The Kohari were not so good about getting out of *their* way."

Beka nodded. "Those battering rams were a great idea. I

wonder if there is some way to fit one to a canoe." He lapsed into silence for a moment, perhaps thinking on a solution. "Oh, how about one between the hulls of a double canoe!"

"I thought the boats were able to get out of the way," I said. Normally, I would not intrude on men's talk of war, but that seemed somewhat obvious.

Beka considered this and shrugged. "Perhaps. Anyway, I think it was the bows of Gordie's men that truly won the day." He turned to the younger man. "We must convince your father to use them more."

"Lord Naio may have recognized that himself," said Ulani. "He saw the same battle as you."

"That is so. Gordie has big crossbows on some of his boats. It takes the strength of two men to draw them back."

"And they will put an arrow right through those Kohari boats," said Mouiri.

"Tear 'em right up," Beka agreed. He turned to the boy like he was imparting a secret. "Says he's going to fix some up to throw rocks instead of arrows!"

Mouiri seemed to think that a quite good idea. I could see him picturing splintered Kohari boats in his head.

"We outnumbered them, in truth," admitted Beka. "I am sure they expected to meet only Gordie's forces and maybe to surprise those. Not a great Mora fleet!"

Marareta nodded knowingly. He perhaps suspected this. "I would take it few escaped."

Lord Beka's lightheartedness disappeared. "We could have slain them all, had we chosen, slaughtered every man. I hadn't the stomach for that."

"Some needed to get home to warn others not to come!" Mouiri reminded him.

"That is so." Beka nodded rather solemnly. "I would as soon fight no more wars."

"The Kohari will forget in a few years," commented Ulani. "They always do."

"Then we have a few years of peace, and that is a good thing," Marareta said. "How soon do you return to your brother, Beka?"

The big man shrugged. "No hurry. Can you put up with me for a day or two?"

"As long as you wish. And as long as the beer lasts!" Both men laughed. "You know that."

"When you go," Ulani said, "I think I shall travel with you. It is time I too spoke with Lord Poneiva." He turned to Toare who had remained politely quiet throughout all this. "You had best remain here till I return or call for you."

He turned his eyes then to me. "Perhaps I shall come back with Lord Gordie. He should be passing south sooner or later."

"So he promised." Beka frowned at us over his bowl. "The man recognizes that the way to his house is no longer a secret. There is concern about smaller raiding parties finding it." He tipped the vessel up and drank long, draining it of beer.

Yes, that was the Kohari way. Men would still seek heads and plunder, despite their great defeat. One could not pretend otherwise. "He will have to control the Gurang now," I muttered, speaking mostly to myself.

"A day I long thought would come," replied Marareta, not much louder.

30. Goings and Comings

BEKA TARRIED TWO days, lazing on the taona's porch and speaking of bygone days. Of all those who had come from the sea with Marareta, Beka was the closest to him, his greatest friend. And, too, I think perhaps Lord Beka looked up to the taona, the man who had led them here — a reluctant leader but a leader none the less, when needed.

Then he was gone, taking young Mouiri with him. The boy was amusing, sometimes playing the warrior with Toare, sometime playing the child with his cousin Tita. He had but three or four years on her and was willing to join her games.

And sometimes I got the feeling he wished I were not also his cousin! No matter; some noble girl would surely take him in hand one of these days. I would assume Lady Pua had all sorts of choices in mind.

Messengers from the High King told us that Gordie had started south, gave us reports of his progress. Almost, I did not want to know, hoped that he might suddenly show up unannounced.

"Gordie is with Poneiva," Marareta announced one evening. "Or was with him. How long he might have tarried, I have not yet heard."

"They could have much to discuss," I said. "There was little opportunity the first time he visited."

"But he was told of the attempt to take Malee. That might hurry him here."

Not just 'might,' I realized. Gordie was surely rushing to us. Perhaps he would outstrip the messengers!

Nearly he did. The man sent to tell us he was on his way arrived less than a day's span before our visitors themselves. Six men arrived after the evening torches were lit, in two small canoes — Gordie, Pahe, and four warriors. I noted the suspected spy, the young Mora Ri'i, was among them. It made sense that Gordie would wish to keep an eye on him.

Seven men I had expected. No time to think on that; Malee went rushing to her father's arms, to be carried to the House of Marareta.

I fell in beside Pahe. "Did not Ulani come with you?" I whispered.

"The bard accompanied us as far as his mother's house. We left him on the shore and paddled on, for Lord Gordie was in a great hurry." His eyes went to the man he loved and served. "He said he would follow."

Late it was, and there was no feasting nor talk that night, only the finding of beds for our weary newcomers. Gordie himself chose to share Oorto's chamber, though he ended up falling asleep in mine, Malee still in his arms.

Follow, Ulani did, but not without sending a messenger ahead. "The Lady Pua comes with him," Marareta told me the next morning. "Poneiva wants her opinion on things."

Though Pua was no longer the power she once had been, a leader of her party, sister of the High King Maitoa, mother to the High King Ve'eta, the current High King did value her advice. "Your house will be very full, Taona," I said. It was not unusual for the two of us to the be first to seek breakfast in the mornings. Oh, Oorto rose even earlier but sought spiritual sustenance first.

That was good because I could let him watch Malee while I filled my stomach. Others drifted out onto the porch to find food. Not everyone in the house — bowls and baskets were carried here and there for those who preferred to eat in their own chambers. Communal meals were also served out near the house of the warriors, shared by them and many of the servants and workers here. At times, Toare ate there.

Malee was still in his arms when Gordie joined us. Which one refused to let go, I am not sure! "My daughter has been telling me of Maratoa," he said, taking a place on our mat. "Is it so that he is responsible for her rescue?"

"Among others," said Marareta.

"Others? You mean Toare," I stated. He deserved credit.

"Yes, I suppose I do," he laughed. "Her two heroes."

"But your son raised the alarm."

"It is so." The taona was willing to say no more.

"Let us get you some food, Malee," I said. "And a bowl for your father too."

By the time we returned to our mat — Malee had insisted on choosing one piece of every type of fruit for Gordie's bowl — Marareta had gone. "I am told this boy is much like his mother," said Gordie, nibbling at a bit of not quite ripe papaya. "I met her when they returned from across the mountains."

"Rahaita," I said. "Not his birth mother, you know."

"But related, right? Some priestess?"

"Pana'a, leader of the priestesses at A'auwa. She was Rahaita's aunt." Rahaita I had never met, slain before I came to this land, but Pana'a I knew fairly well. "The boy is like her but also like his father."

"Marareta is a good man to be like," said Gordie. He turned to his daughter. "You must introduce me to the brave Maratoa."

She giggled greatly at this.

"You still wish to travel south?" I asked. "You would meet Pana'a there."

"There is no reason to change my plan. We can spend some time there and then return to finish my business with Poneiva." Gordie sat a while without speaking, perhaps thinking on that business, before saying, "I think it might be a good idea to see more of this land of the Mora before deciding anything."

"And what do you think of it so far, oh Lord of the North?"

He laughed at the title. "They do call me that, don't they? It frightens me a little, Ranadi. They are a numerous people and their

112

land is rich. I passed through the northwest corner quickly, many years ago, on my way to — to my home, thinking of nothing but that. Now I shall have my eyes more open." He smiled at a thought. "And you will be along to make sure I miss nothing."

I had assumed I would accompany him. "Malee?" I asked.

"Yes. She too should begin learning of the Mora."

Malee was learning of many things. We could speak of those later. For now it was enough that her father was here.

Would that were enough for me.

Part III. A'auwa

31. Crowded

Pua we had expected, and Ulani. That Ma'ave and Aeta would accompany them, we had not. Three canoes they filled, with their attendants and guards.

"I think I shall sleep in the house of the taona's warriors," Toare whispered to me. "So there is more room for the guests, you understand." He knew I did.

"But will one of them share your bed?" How could I not ask?

Malee was making it her duty to fill in Maratoa about our visitors. "That is Aeta," she told him. "She's my friend. And 'er mommy, Ma-vay." She took a look at Pua and then up at me. "Is Pua 'er mommy too?"

"She's Aeta's grandmother," I explained. Did she know what that meant? "Ma'ave's mommy."

"Oh. A crocodile ate my grandmother." She looked again at our guests, gathering their belongings, preparing to walk to the House of Marareta. "Ma-vay should marry Daddy. Then Pua could be my grandmother too!"

"I know Lady Pua," claimed Maratoa. "She's a friend of my father."

"And a very important woman," Toare told him. "It appears they are ready."

Rika led the procession to the house, chatting with Pua all the way. Old friends, it seemed, though he was a commoner. Unlike his friend Hito, Rika had never felt an ambition to elevate himself to the nobility; he had been content with serving Marareta ever since returning with him from beyond the mountains. Ever since he had put aside a life as a warrior.

For he was a warrior, Rika, though he was now the taona's attendant, and a husband and father. For some, moving from one life to another is easy. For some, happiness comes.

Marareta came out on his entry porch as we approached the house. "Welcome, Lady Pua," he called out. "Welcome all!" That was about as far as the taona was willing to go with greeting a crowd of guests. He was not an outgoing man.

We had fallen in beside Ulani, without speaking. "We descend as a great crowd on the taona," mused the bard. "I think he would rather forget politics."

"He has tried," replied Toare. "You know that well, Master."

"I do, Toare, I do. But the Mora people will not forget their Hero from the Sea." Ulani watched Pua and Marareta disappear into the house. "My own epics may have something to do with that."

It took some time to settle everyone into that crowded house. I stayed out of the way, taking both Malee and Maratoa to my own chamber to play and then nap. I think I drowsed as well, for Oorto was there suddenly and I did not remember him coming in!

"Our guests gather on the south porch," he told me. "I have no desire to take part in that but you might." Oorto glanced at a yawning Maratoa. "I can stay with the young ones. I brought food for them." He held up a full bowl.

Why not? Oorto probably didn't want me there anyway. I slipped out and down the hall, through the gathering room, where a pair of servant busied themselves with cleaning, and out to the porch. Pua made a space between herself and Ma'ave as soon as she spied me. I might have felt more comfortable taking the place below her daughter; there was no reason to make Ma'ave resent me.

Pua was speaking. "We are here to speak for the High King, at least in some part." She waved a broad hand toward Ulani. "I and my son."

Gordie nodded. "Then I will listen to your words, Lady Pua. I have had little time to speak with Poneiva in depth. I keep needing to rush off elsewhere as soon as I arrive."

"In truth, I have little to say. Poneiva but wishes us to speak of things that might be, and to learn your thoughts."

"Some of them, perhaps," replied Gordie. "And some will become known to the High King when we speak again." From the corner of my eye, I glimpsed Ma'ave's nod of approval. She looked like she might have wanted to say something, too, but held her tongue.

"As is to be expected," said Pua. "Some tell him you should become a tenth king of the Mora, joining your lands to ours. This he would not approve unless all nine kings agreed."

"I doubt Mahutunoa would be in favor," said Ulani.

Gordie was not so certain. "He might have the most to gain, especially were I to recognize his ownership of the hills and of the passes."

The bard considered this. "So might it be," he admitted.

"But I am not sure I would want my people to be under Mora rule. Better, perhaps, I remain independent, and call myself what I will. Lord? King? It makes no difference."

"Or 'pungay' like a lord of the Kohari," I suggested.

He screwed up his face at that idea. "I think I prefer cap'n. Cap'n Gordie. Yes, Captain Gordon Watkins, commander of the grandest fleet on the Gurang!" Both he and Marareta laughed uproariously at this but I fear no others understood the joke.

For some time, our attention turned to filling our stomachs and little of import was said. Questions of family, of children. Speculation on the crops and arguments as to whether this rainy season was wetter than last year. Talk about the inconveniences of travel.

This last led Gordie to ask, "You will travel to A'auwa with us, Lady Pua?"

"No, I no longer make long journeys. I shall send Ma'ave in my stead." The younger woman's eyebrows shot up. It seemed it was the first she had heard of this! "You will do well, my daughter." Pua regarded Ulani across the bowls and baskets. "My son may go too. I do not try to guess as to what schemes he and the High King might have."

Marareta chuckled. "As I did not try to guess at the schemes of you and Lord Hareata, my lady. Yet I could not avoid getting tangled up in them."

"And we are all the better for it, Taona," she replied.

32. Pursuers

A NAP WAS all I wanted. An hour or two on a slow, gray afternoon. I had gone to the less-used north porch to find some privacy. It was not to be.

Toare came up out of the drizzle, dripping onto the rough floor. "Do you know anything of Gordie's man Ri'i?" he asked, at once. Not even a greeting!

Best I not say too much, maybe. "I know that he is a Mora who showed up at the trade village months ago. He would say nothing of his past."

The young bard lowered himself beside me, looking out at the warriors' practice fields. "He raises my suspicions. Ri'i wanders off alone sometimes, taking care that none see him."

"But you do." Obviously. I suppose Toare heard a trace of mockery in my words, for he smiled at them.

"I watch him now, trying to learn what his purpose is."

I hesitated, but why should Toare not know all I did? Who could I better trust than this boy? "Pahe suspects him of being a spy." There.

"Ah." He popped back up again. "Then I would do well to continue watching."

With that he was off, dashing somewhere through the rain. To the house of the warriors, perhaps. This porch was where Marareta would meet sometimes with his warriors and workers. Now it was again deserted so I returned to my interrupted nap.

Well it was I slept, for Marareta feasted his guests that night. Yesterday, they had rested after their journey, and most seemed none too eager to exert themselves this morning. But they would feast. They were Mora, after all.

In Marareta's common room, the central chamber of his house — as in most houses of noble Mora — we feasted, and then the taona told all that Ulani would present some epic or another on the south porch. Not the one of Marareta's journey over the mountains and certainly not the one of the civil war that followed; there was too much personal sorrow for the taona in that one. "I shall sing of the High King Maitoa when he was young," Ulani announced. "One of Master Isa's poems." To sing of Pua's brother was a good choice. The man had been a hero, a warrior, in his youth.

"I have heard enough of my master's voice," Toare whispered to me. "I think I'll go walk in the taona's gardens."

It sounded like a good idea. "So shall I," I said, and followed him into the scented night. Among the citrus trees we wandered, out beyond the light of the torches, where only stars showed the way.

Toare, I allowed to lead. There was no place I much wanted to go so it did not matter. Of a sudden, he placed a hand on my arm. "Shh."

I was momentarily annoyed. I had not been saying anything! Then I followed his eyes. A form was slipping through the trees, a little ahead of us. "Ri'i?" I whispered.

"Stay here," Toare commanded.

I might have laughed or maybe I successfully stifled it. Either way, I was not going to let this boy tell me what to do! He only glanced at me as I fell in behind him, and went on, following Ri'i.

Toward the river the man was going. Stealthily, keeping to the shadows, but not in any seeming haste. In a few minutes, he was on the path between Teoma and the House of Marareta. We continued to trail Ri'i, at a distance.

His head came up, alert to something we did not see. Quickly, the warrior slipped into the trees beside the path. We did the same. A form was furtively moving up the trail. I could make out nothing of his features. He too was keeping to shadows!

The stranger passed by, not too far from us, and Ri'i followed behind, even more stealthy in his movements than before. Then

120

came we, pursuing one who pursued. This was a great puzzle to me and surely to my companion as well.

First one man, then the other, left the pathway and passed northward through an orchard. I did not like the idea of either of us following them into it. "I will go find some of the taona's warriors," I said to Toare. "Be careful."

Surely the boy would go after them. It would be unlike Toare not to. Not far was it to the front porch and a pair of men loitered there, supposedly on guard. "Toare is following two strange men. Over, um, there." I pointed in what I thought the proper direction. "Someone should be alerted."

One immediately responded, saying to his fellow, "I'll go to the captain." Off he ran, around the north end of the house.

"You had best stay here, my lady," the other told me. Almost I did — but could not.

"I'll go to the north porch," I said. Maybe I would. First, anyway. By the time I reached it, a knot of warriors came trotting by, brought out of their house by my report. I saw no reason not to go in their wake. They would keep me safe!

A noise ahead, thrashing somewhere among the trees. The warriors rushed forward, then halted. One held a torch aloft so we might see three men, standing glaring at one another. "These two were sneaking about in the night," declared Toare.

"And what were you doing?" asked the unknown man, looking from one to the other. "Lurking in the dark and up to no good, I would think." I was not sure if he was being serious.

"I did no wrong," insisted Ri'i. "I followed this stranger who approached the house!"

That man dropped his arms to his sides, apparently resigned to his discovery and capture, and said no more. Not a young man was he, blocky of build, square of face.

The captain of Marareta's warriors looked from one to the other. What was his name? Heva?

"We need to take you both to the taona," he said, "and get this figured out!"

33. Revelations

"RI'I SERVES ME," said Ulani. "Which is to say he serves the High King." Even Pua seemed surprised by that. I suspected that Poneiva had no idea this man even existed, much less served him.

"To spy on me?" Gordie seemed amused rather than angry.

"And to watch for dangers. There have been rumors of conspiracies and threats against you for years." He turned to the stranger, frowning. "And now it seems we have prevented one, maybe."

"I am but a messenger, Master Ulani," spoke the man, "bearing words for Lord Gordie." He spread his arms. "I am a threat to no one."

"And who would send a messenger secretly?" asked Gordie, stepping forward.

"Ah, a friend in the north, my lord. Perhaps I should not speak the name among these Mora?"

"Hidlat? I hide nothing from those here."

"So it is," the messenger said.

Ulani sounded doubtful of all this. "How does a Kohari enter the homeland of the Mora?"

"One might land on the Salt Coast and cross over the hills," the man said, quite matter of factly, "That has been done in the past. Attempted, anyway. Simpler was to come to the Great Falls as a Kohari trader and then assume a Mora identity. Cut my hair, exchange my kilt for a loincloth, uncover my tattoos." His hand went to a small design on his left arm. "Anyone who looks Mora can climb the ropes unchallenged."

"But you also sound and act Mora," said Gordie. His voice held a certain amount of approval, I think.

"I am of mixed blood. My mother was a Mora woman — from a family of fishers — and my father a trader of the Kohari."

It was Pua who observed, "Then by our laws you are Mora."

"And by Kohari laws I am Kohari. I have lived long as a trader and know both worlds." He gave us a sly smile. "This is not my first time to walk above the Great Falls."

Gordie nodded at this and turned to Ri'i. "So what shall I do with you?"

The young man shot a sidelong look at Ulani before replying, "I shall depart if you wish, Lord Gordie."

"You have kept better watch than some who truly served me. If you and Ulani are willing, I would have you stay with us on this journey." His voice became almost imperceptibly firmer. "But not when we return home."

Ulani only shrugged. "Stay with Gordie if you wish, Ri'i. But go now, while we speak of other things."

As the young warrior departed, curious eyes were turned to the Kohari messenger. "Call me Ti'ine, lords of the Mora," spoke the man. "My name among the Kohari you need not know."

"So what message do you bear?" asked Gordie. "Speak freely before my friends."

"It is your friends that worry my masters, Lord Gordie. After the destruction of our fleet, they worry about an alliance between you and the Mora." His eyes swept around the room before returning to Gordie. "This makes them hesitant to take any actions."

"And they do wish to take actions?"

"The Kohari nation is in disarray. Some see this as the chance to break the rule of the priests." I think the man would have spat after saying 'priests,' had he not been in Marareta's house. "Let them serve their god, Hidlat says, and let men rule men."

"But they fear upsetting things right now," spoke Marareta. He smiled. "The mighty King of the Gurang is an unknown."

Gordie and he laughed at that — again, they were the only two sharing their joke.

"Lord Habaccan speaks of raising one up to be high king of the Kohari, to unify our people against threats from the outside."

"The inside too, I would think," observed the taona. "A Kohari high king could deal with the power of the Temple of Mihasa."

"Would we wish such a thing?" asked Pua. "Better the Kohari remain divided!" She gave Ti'ine a respectful nod. "You understand this, I am sure."

"I do, my lady." He turned his attention back to Gordie. "I was sent only to tell you what was on the minds of your friends in the north. This and no more, save to bear any words you might have back to them."

"I have none, right now. Perhaps you, too, should travel with us until I find some you could carry home."

"As the Lord Gordie wishes," replied Ti'ine.

34. Preparations

"I DO NOT like the Mora woman," Pahe confided to me. I could have pretended ignorance but I knew he meant Ma'ave.

"You do not have to," I replied. "You are not marrying her."

"That is fortunate! Were I the sort to have a wife, I would prefer one like you, maybe."

"Ah, Pahe, I have my own faults. I am given to ambitions and intrigues." Maybe that laid it on too thick, but I knew I could be selfish. Sometimes I wondered if I wanted too much, if I made things difficult for myself without reason.

"You are loyal. That is enough." As was he. Perhaps Pahe saw that as the greatest virtue. "Lady Ma'ave's little girl is a sweet child," he said, turning our conversation elsewhere.

"The lady changes her mind day to day whether to send Aeta home or bring her with us."

"Malee would miss her."

I must laugh at that. "Maybe. But she would miss Malee more."

"I understand that Ulani will leave with Lady Pua." He paused for but a moment. "I think I do like the bard." Was there something in his voice? Ulani and Pahe? No, surely not.

"And then he will travel on to speak with the High King. Ulani says he will try to rejoin us later." After a second or two, I thought to add, "He is leaving his apprentice with us."

One of those well-known scowls appeared on Pahe's face. "He spends too much time looking at you!"

Did he? Many men do — I would be fool not to know this. But I thought Toare was over his boyhood crush. I returned from my moment of reverie to watch Pahe go down to the edge of Teoma to help push a laden canoe out into the flow. Of course, he had decided I should accept Gordie's proposal, marry his master. Most days, I did not even think of this, so many other things were in my head.

Surely if I loved the man, it would not be so. Would it? "I return to the house," I called. Pahe was keeping himself busy, helping the taona's men. He was not one who cared to be idle.

Two days. Then we would be on our way up the river, on our way to A'auwa. I suspected I would not wish to leave once I was there. Men and women passed me on the path, bearing baskets of fruit. The produce of Marareta's groves was traded far up and down Teoma, and even Teiri.

There was Oorto before the House of Marareta, with Maratoa and Malee and, yes, little Aeta and Rahiri as well. Tita sat on the steps, watching their games without much interest. She was of an age when boys tended to crowd into ones thoughts.

None of that for me, when I was becoming a young woman! It was not permitted in the temple. I missed much of childhood. Had I not escaped with Hito I might have missed life altogether.

Rahiri jumped up from whatever they were playing at in the dirt and ran to me. "I'm coming too! I'm coming too! Mommy says so!"

I turned to Oorto. "To A'auwa?"

"The whole family is going," he replied. "They are going to leave Tita in charge here." The girl looked up, gave a slight smile, and returned to whatever daydreams were occupying her.

"Panoha? Isn't that — awkward?"

"Because of Pana'a? She knows well of her husband's love for the priestess. It is no different than him having a second wife." Except the Priestesses of the Isle were not permitted to marry.

He looked at little Rahiri. "And the priestess should be allowed to gaze upon the child who was named for her."

I knew of this. Hito had told me Rahiri was Pana'a's birth name, changed when she became chief priestess and assumed the name of the sacred waterfall, as had those who came before her. Panoha knew this too, I assumed. Well, no matter. Mora ways are strange; I am sure both Oorto and I could agree on this. Maybe Pahe, too.

"Let's go get some lunch," I said. "Ho, not through the house. Go around." Oorto and I followed the crowd of youngsters around the house to the south porch. Tita remained on the steps; where exactly her mind was, I could not tell you.

It was early for lunch, but children are always hungry. And so was I! There were few on the porch in the late morning but over against the wall sat Toare and Ma'ave in deep conversation about something. Had they renewed their affair? Not that it mattered any to me. Toare could do as he chose.

"Let's eat down here on the grass," I told the group, though we were halfway up the steps. "I'll go up and get some bowls." It took two armfuls to bring enough, while Oorto entertained the little ones.

"Aeta needs to poop," said Malee, as soon as I sat down.

Rahiri giggled. "Be nice," Maratoa told his little sister. "Aeta is our guest."

"You should be nice anyway," I said. "Come along, dear." The Mora have rather strict rules about where one may relieve oneself. Otherwise I would have taken little Aeta behind the nearest tree.

"Are you still sure you want a large family?" asked Oorto on our return.

Did I even need to think about it? "Quite large, Friend Oorto. Five girls and five big brothers to protect them."

"I can protect myself!" proclaimed Rahiri, sticking out her tongue at her own big brother.

Maratoa's dignity would not allow him to acknowledge her. After all, he was going to be a great warrior. "How go your lessons, Oorto?" I asked, lowering my voice.

"Well enough, considering the turmoil in this house." His dark eyes rested on Maratoa and Malee in turn. "I teach them little ways to keep the mind from — from wandering where it is not safe. For now, that is enough."

Little did I understand of this but I knew it was best that the children be prepared for what might come in their lives. "It must be a little like the disciplines I learned at their age, when first training at the temple. Only later did we use them, put them together, and learn to dance."

Oorto smiled at this. "Perhaps it is, Ranadi. I've never learned to dance, myself."

When we took the children inside for their naps, Ma'ave and Toare were gone.

35. Starting Out

MANY CANOES. WE were like a fleet going off to war!

Yes, I have seen a fleet going off to war, Gordie when he went to fight the Kohari that first time. I do know what I am talking about. Anyway, we were many canoes, filled by the taona and his family and a dozen retainers or more — I never managed to come up with an exact number — and all those who had traveled with Gordie and with me. Save the two warriors Poneiva had sent with us; those had already left with Pua and Ulani, headed back to the House of the High King.

Ma'ave and her daughter and attendants filled spaces in the canoes, too, and Toare, once again left to his own devices. He need not have come along had he not wished. He owed nothing to any of us. Or did he choose to come because of Ma'ave? I had been too busy to pay any attention to those two, knew not whether they shared a sleeping mat or anything else.

Past the mouth of Teiri we stroked, heading southward, up Teoma's stream. Perhaps I should not say 'we' stroked, for my attention was on Malee, in my charge. Four small children were scattered among these canoes and each needed watching.

Oh, I skipped someone — Ti'ine. The Kohari who was also a Mora paddled with the rest of us, but spoke little. I felt his eyes on me, at times. Maybe Lord Hidlat had told him of who I was. Maybe he just liked to look at beautiful women, eh?

I remembered well the place we encamped that first night. Toare did, too, for he sat down beside me, saying, "A year and more has it been since we slept here."

"But this time no men will attempt to kidnap me, mistaking me for Teme," I replied. They must not have had a good description for she is a head taller than me.

"It will be good to see Ruiru again," he said. "He has built a shrine by A'auwa, I hear."

I only nodded. His mother was there, too, with Hito. Maybe that was his reason for joining our journey.

But Ruiru — he had shared our trip south then, sent as bodyguard by Teme's brother, the High King Poneiva. Too, he had shared her journey to the north, and her adventures there, while I remained at the House of Arierona. A priest of Wenatu now, the god of the rainbow, he was.

"There is food. Come and join us," he said, rising. I had plopped down here, weary, but knew I should eat. Malee, as well, must be tended to, though she was with her father now.

I sat down with the group gathered around the taona. Dried fish and meat, there was, and plentiful fresh fruit. "Tita will do well," Panoha was saying. "She has Hepetea and Rika to run things properly for her."

"I hope so," responded Marareta. He did not seem so sure of it.

I took a seat on the ground at Ma'ave's left. No desire had I to assert a higher status by going to her right. We were essentially equals, cousins. She glanced at me and turned back to Panoha, saying, "Tita is a sensible girl. She reminds me of my mother." A crooked smile. "Maybe a little too much."

There were murmurs of agreement. "She does take after her father's side of the family," admitted Panoha. "Your family."

"Our Rahiri, on the other hand," said Marareta, "reminds me sometimes too much of her Uncle Hareata."

"That would not be a bad thing," murmured Ma'ave. "He was a great leader."

"He and your mother saved this Mora nation," said Marareta.

"You had some part in that, Husband," Panoha said.

Hareata — that was Panoha's brother. I knew the name only from the epic poems. He was said to be wise but devious. Not at all like his open and honest sister!

And Toare was his son. He had taken a seat across from me;

131

with Ulani gone, Gordie elsewhere, he had the place at Marareta's right hand, the highest noble. Not that Marareta cared one way or another. Here, perhaps, no one cared. I thought of Toare, most of the time, as but a boy who made up songs. He was much more than this. Toare could have been a commander of warriors, had he chosen, captain to some great noble or king, married well. Married a woman with power, like the one at my side.

"I should go look after Malee," I said, rising.

Ma'ave stood as well. "Aeta is with her. I'll come along."

Both girls slept, close to where Malee's father sat in one of the open shelters, conversing in a low voice with some traders. "Best to just leave them," I whispered. "This is probably as good a place as any to sleep myself." There had been light rain on and off. Over maybe, but the ground was damp.

Ma'ave looked around. "It probably is," she agreed. "I'll unroll my mat here too."

People were settling down all around us, those of our party, other travelers on the river. Had someone posted sentries? I yawned. Of course, Gordie and Marareta would think to do that. Don't worry about it.

"You have known Toare a long time," came Ma'ave's voice across the darkness.

"Since I first came to the land of the Mora," I replied. "He was at the House of Marareta when Hito took me there."

There was silence for some time. Had she fallen asleep?

"I knew him as Ulani's apprentice, but fate had placed our feet on different paths. That changed a season ago."

"And now?" I asked.

"We are no longer lovers," she said. "We both felt that best, at least for now."

"While you travel." I assumed that was her meaning.

"Travel, yes. But more than that. Things change for both of us.

For all of us, maybe I should say. Whether life will carry us further apart or back together, only the gods know."

"And the priestesses at A'auwa." I was not too sleepy to make a little joke.

"Hmm, I must think to ask them of it." Then, I think Ma'ave did fall asleep. But I did not.

She snored terribly. I don't know how Toare put up with it.

36. River to Road

"If enemies mean you mischief, this seems a good time for it," said Toare.

"Not at all," felt Pahe. "We are on guard when we travel but they might expect us to relax when we reach our destination."

"Then we had best just keep watch all the time," was Gordie's response. "We still have no idea who wished to harm me." His eyes went to his daughter, playing on the pebbly beach with her friends. "Or take Malee."

"If it was even the same enemy," Pahe said. I think he saw enemies everywhere, eager to harm his master. Especially in this strange land!

Days had we traveled up Teoma, and nights had we slept by its flow. That was not too strong, for the rainy season had not yet flooded streams and lakes. Now we halted at the first falls, the place where our trip would abandon river and take to road.

I walked down to where the children waded, below the falls. This cataract was not high nor impressive, but a canoe could not pass it.

"It is not so great a river," remarked Pahe, who had come to stand beside me.

"Greater than the one by your master's house," I had to point out. But, of course, dwarfed by the Gurang. "Perhaps you will be more impressed by A'auwa."

"We shall see." He looked about. "Who rules here?"

"This is the northern end of Arierona's kingdom," I told him. "We have been traveling through that of Avatu."

"Avatu," he repeated. "But Marareta does not serve him." Pahe sounded uncertain of his statement.

"The House of Marareta lies near the southern edge of the kingdom of Va'aru."

"Ah. I have heard of him. He controls the trade with the Kohari."

That was so. His house lay near the Great Falls and the sea. "The Lady Panoha is a cousin of Va'aru. Had she a son, he would be a candidate for the king's dais someday."

"We must urge Marareta to spend more time with his wife!"

It was rare to see Pahe smile, much less jest. "So we should," I laughed. "But a son of Tita or Rahiri would also be in the royal line."

He frowned then; not quite a scowl but it was close. "Yes, Ranadi. I know how Mora inheritance goes." Too well did he know!

We slept to the serenade of the rushing water that night, and set forth on the much trodden road come morning. There would be a long walk — more than the legs of the little ones could handle. Even Maratoa, though he insisted he was able to keep up with any other warrior.

Plenty enough arms could carry them; that was no problem. And all the adults were healthy and able to walk. No litters would be necessary. "I fear the Lady Pua no longer has the legs for such a journey," Marareta confided to me. "Once she and I walked great distances together and I was the one who had trouble keeping up." There was a sadness in the taona's voice; perhaps he feared losing yet another friend, another he loved. It was said he and Pua had briefly been lovers when first he came to our land.

Why did he say such a thing to me? I think no other would have understood. Not Pua's daughter. Not Marareta's wife. Maybe Oorto would.

It was on the second evening that Ti'ine voiced concern about some of the traders who shared our road. "They hide their tattoos," he said. "Maybe warriors." The man shrugged. "Maybe even priests."

As there was frequent rain, it was not strange that some travelers would wear ponchos of woven fiber. Not strange to me, anyway. But he might be right — and every time now a man so covered approached, I felt wary, and maybe gripped Malee's hand more tightly!

This road was well-traveled and we were numerous. Surely, none would attempt mischief, I told myself. Not here, not now. I realized that spies, however, might be among those who walked the road to A'auwa. Not just 'might,' perhaps.

Pahe and Ti'ine — these two had become comradely, often walking together. Not friends, I am sure, but with common interests and concerns. They would talk of many things, talk in the pidgin. Sometimes, I walked with them, only listening, not joining their conversations, to break the monotony of our trudge. I think maybe my Kohari birth led the two to speak freely before me.

"I do not want my master to have closer ties to the Mora either. What need has he of them?" Pahe was saying, as I came even with them. A frequent subject for the two, that was.

"Neither needs the other," agreed Ti'ine. "The Kohari, however, might benefit from his friendship now."

"Which Kohari?" asked Pahe. "Lord Gordie would not become involved in your factions."

I spoke up. "Marareta told me how his enemy Nezama once thought to gather a force of masterless men and go make himself a king of the Kohari."

"I have heard of him," said Ti'ine. "He is named in one of the epic poems, is he not?"

"The one where Marareta crossed the mountains," Pahe informed him. "I heard Ulani sing it."

"He composed it," I informed him, "using Oorto's account."

Pahe nodded slowly, his face expressionless. "The shaman never spoke to me of that journey."

"He would see it through different eyes than a Mora," opined Ti'ine. A low laugh. "As, Lady Rahiniti, I am sure you saw your own journey across the mountains differently than the warrior Hito."

136

"Ah, it is too late to set the account straight there," I sighed. "Hito told his version to Toare and Ulani, and so it is."

Both chuckled, taking that in the spirit in which I had spoken it. "At least your name is mentioned," spoke Ti'ine. "Most of we who serve loyally will be forgotten."

"True," agreed Pahe, "but I do not mind." He squinted up the road, as we marched forward through patches of shade and morning sun. "Those traders ahead of us have been gradually falling back," he observed.

Ti'ine glanced their direction. "So they have." I could see the men; colorless ponchos of woven grass covered their shoulders. My companions almost imperceptibly began to speed up their pace. But we had overtaken other travelers on this road, passed them by. Why concern over these three traders?

The slope dropped off steeply to our right, into a deep tree-filled ravine. Forest lay thick on our left. We were in one of those spots where the road rose; oh, it had been slowly rising all along, ever since we left the falls, but there were more hills now as we grew nearer to A'auwa's basin.

A good place for an ambush, I realized of a sudden, a place where men could strike and run, with a chance of escape.

A shouted warning — as one, Ti'ine and Pahe sprinted forward.

37. Lives Lost

STONE KNIVES FLASHED in the hands of the strangers, as they wheeled toward Gordie. There were guards, yes, but only one stood between the assassins and their target. That man grappled the foremost assailant, having time not even to lay his hand on the Mora club dangling at his waist. The other two darted around the struggling pair.

Enough time it was to allow Gordie to grasp his own knife, standing ready for an attack. The man who stood beside him, the man with whom he had been conversing while we walked, did not stand ready. War-club in hand, he leaped forward.

Marareta, I realized. I also realized I was running toward them. Why? I halted to gather myself, to take in what was happening. Now Pahe and Ti'ine were there, ready to fight. Other warriors rushed to join them. A woman's voice cried out. "Keep watch! There may be others!" Ma'ave, surely. It took a cool head to think of such things in the confusion of an encounter.

And if there were others, they would surely target Malee. I started toward the girl and was relieved to see a pair of warriors doing the same. My eyes went back to the fight.

I had not known the taona was so fierce a fighter, and so skilled with the club. This weapon, favored by many Mora, is a flattened piece of heavy wood or stone, used as much to thrust as to swing. Marareta very much preferred to thrust, it seemed. He lunged forward, catching one of the men full in the chest and sending him toppling into the dirt.

Another man was already lying in the road, the first warrior to attempt stopping these assassins. Now one attacker was slashing at Gordie with a quartz knife. Gordie was no fighting man. I knew this. He did not take time to train with weapons, other than occasionally casting a Diwarna bamboo spear. Usually at fish in the river!

He parried clumsily, backing away. Ah, Marareta had turned

and swung his club in a wide arc, ending at the back of the attacker's head. He crumpled and did not rise again. Ever.

And the third man was down too, knifed by Pahe, I think. If there were others, they chose not to show themselves. It had seemed a desperate attempt, to attack here on the road, with so many in our company. What sort of men would act so?

"This one has priestly tattoos," said Toare, peering at the man whose skull Marareta had broken.

"But few signs on the others," spoke the taona. "Common warriors, maybe. This one still breathes." It was the man he had caught with his thrusting attack. Marareta squatted beside him. "His breast bone is crushed." The man's breath was rasping, labored.

Marareta rose. "We'll get nothing from him. Best to end his suffering." He paid no more attention to the man but turned to the fallen Mora. "Ri'i," he said. "May the gods receive him."

I know not who dispatched the wounded attacker. I do not think I want to know. The three fallen attackers were buried beside the road. I would have tossed them in the ravine, but that is not the Mora way. Ri'i's body was to be carried with us until a more proper burial site was found. That the boy should rest by some shrine, even by A'auwa itself, was only right.

As we again set out, Gordie and I fell in beside Marareta. "I had heard you were become a warrior and hero," Gordie said. "I am not sure I quite believed it until now."

"It was not by choice," replied the taona. His hand went unconsciously to the mark of Teva on his left shoulder. "As Hito, I became a priest, intending to leave such things behind." A sigh of resignation. "It seems I can not."

"I brought this to you," said Gordie. "That man who tried to knife me was a priest, you said?"

"Of Te'eta. His rose quartz blade would have identified him even if his tattoos did not."

139

"A sacrificial knife. I know about that." Gordie's smile seemed rather bleak. "I might even have sold the quartz for it. Weren't his followers involved in the civil war here?"

"Many who led the rebels served the God of the Red Sky. As to this priest who attacked you, who can say?"

There was no answer for that, and both men strode forward in silence. I tired of such company soon, and dropped back to walk with Toare. He had his own opinions. "This attack feels the work of fanatics," he said. "Men who were willing to die if they could accomplish their goal."

What goal might that be? Oh, yes, to kill Gordie, I know this. But to what purpose?

"I wish the children had not seen this," I said.

"They saw little," Toare replied. "Aeta and Rahiri, anyway. Maratoa, I fear, will be boasting of his father for some time."

And Malee had already experienced violence up close when men had attempted to kidnap her. She seemed unperturbed now, walking along with the rest of us. "The taona is a fighting man," I said. "I had not known this."

"Then you have not listened to my poems!" the boy responded. "But I know what you mean, Rahiniti. Marareta seems a man of peace. He *is* a man of peace."

All I could say was, "I hope he finds it."

38. Greetings

I WOULD HAVE liked to turn aside at the Pool of the Moon, showed the high Falls of Pana'a to Gordie, but he was eager to press on to the House of Arierona, only hours further. If I chose to marry him, I decided, I would wed the man here and bathe in the sacred pool, as had Teme and countless brides before her.

"I shall take you to see the falls soon," I promised Malee. "There will be time."

The lake itself was wonder enough for those who had not seen it before. Even for we who had, maybe! Pahe remained impassive but I think he was impressed — at last.

"There is something 'ere," said Malee, as she gazed up the length of A'auwa. "Up there."

"That's where the priestesses live," Maratoa told her. "My mother is one of them. My other mother."

She looked up at me. "Can we go visit 'er?"

"Boys aren't allowed," said Maratoa, sounding none too happy about it.

"Pana'a will surely come to see both of you," I said. "First we shall visit King Arierona and ask if we might stay in his house." A formality. Of course we would stay in the House of Arierona.

"He's my grandfather," announced Maratoa. "My other, other mother's father. My dead mother." I was surprised the boy could sort them all out.

"My grandfather is called Oorloso," Malee informed him. "'E's an elder of 'is tribe."

"That's as good as a king any day," I told her.

It was still early; we should reach the house soon after noon, even at a pace that seemed far too slow to me. I wanted to be back in the only house that truly felt like home to me any more. I admit it; it was not the House of Gordie in which I wished to dwell. Yet I might anyway.

But here by the side of A'auwa felt like home too. I need not be in the king's house for that. The tall pines rose on either side, their scent filling the heavy air — the trees Arierona, and the king before him, had planted for the harvest of timber. The rulers here protected the ancient growth now, trees that might have sprung from the earth before even the Mora came to this land. These stood in patches here and there, and a forest of them grew across the lake, where men built shrines to the gods.

There dwelt Hito, at least at times. I understood Ruiru did so too, now. But in the House of Arierona dwelt Teme and Bafa; more even than Hito, I yearned to again see them. Perhaps Bafa would meet us on the road, as he had when I first journeyed here with Teme, a year past.

Ah, warriors did approach. That was not Bafa at their head, however. Too large. Aranu! I certainly did not mind seeing him either.

"Welcome, travelers!" he called. His eyes went back and forth from the taona to Gordie. I think he was not certain which should be greeted first. "Welcome all." That was one way of solving it. Then he embraced each in turn; something he said low, that I could not hear, in Gordie's ear. That it was words of Demba and his loss, I have little doubt.

I was not willing to be left out of things so I made sure to slip forward, with Malee holding one hand and Maratoa the other. "Report reached us that you had been attacked," Aranu was saying. "Only an hour ago, or I would have been heading north far sooner."

"It is so," said Marareta. "We lost one man."

"Laid to rest near a shrine to one of your gods," added Gordie.

"Babi." Pahe said this. It was simply the first shrine we had reached with Ri'i's body, but the earth goddess seemed appropriate to watch over his remains.

The next few minutes, as we marched south, were filled with a retelling of that encounter. Aranu nodded knowingly at the tale.

"That is the Marareta I knew of old," he said. "The man who fought a great war across the mountains and another here."

"And now may he sleep again," replied the taona. "Is Arierona well?"

"The king – declines. His legs no longer answer to his will and he is often borne in a litter."

I remembered his difficulty in getting up and down when I had first met the man. Had it grown worse while I lived here? I had not paid that much attention to King Arierona, nor had our paths crossed very often. Even though I was his guest.

"He was the first king of the Mora I met when I came to this world," said Marareta. "A great warrior, a commander in a great fleet." He paused. Almost as an afterthought, he said, "And a loving father."

"He does not blame you for what happened to Rahaita," said Aranu. "You know that well."

"No, he does not. But sometimes I do."

Aranu felt it best to turn their talk elsewhere. "Amirea and the girls are eager to see you," he said. "All of you." He craned his neck to look back over our party. "I haven't seen Oorto. Ah, there." He waved toward the shaman, who walked beside the taona's wife. "Oh, and Panoha! It has been long."

So Aranu jabbered nearly until we reached the king's house. One would think him a high-spirited boy rather than one of Arierona's greatest captains.

"Maybe Ponu will come out to greet you," he said. "Don't expect Arierona. But he'll feast you tomorrow, have no fear!"

"Your greeting is enough, Friend Aranu," spoke Marareta. "As I am sure both the king and his nephew know." He turned and called out, "Lady Ma'ave! You might wish to stand with us when we reach the House of Arierona."

She nodded in agreement and walked forward to join us, holding Aeta's hand. But Ponu, nephew and likely heir of the king,

did not await us on the sunlit front porch, nor any other representative. It seemed Aranu was considered quite important enough to
serve in that role.

Ah, wait, someone at the entry — a man, short and somewhat
fat, came forth, smiling.

"It is he who was my husband," said Ma'ave.

39. The House of Bafa

"Daddy!" cried Aeta and ran into her father's arms.

"I did not expect to see you here, Iro," Ma'ave said.

"Nor I you," the man admitted. "My intent was to meet with Lord Gordie and his friends." He laughed easily. "It would seem you are one of those."

"I should have mentioned he was here," mumbled Aranu. "Ho, you," he called to a servant. "Has anyone prepared places for our guests?"

"That is my reason for standing here, Lord Aranu," replied the man, smiling. "Lady Teme asked me show them to their lodging." He looked over the group. "The lady thought you might desire to stay together. Follow me."

We did, not going into the king's house but off to the north and around, past the gardens. Many smaller buildings stood about the House of Arierona, housing retainers and servants, warriors, workers. A village, it was. Aranu, I think, was as ignorant of our destination as we.

"The House of Bafa," announced our guide. Now, I had known Bafa had a separate house; I had lived in it for a season when we were lovers. The man liked to be close to his workshop, which lay a bit further on.

"It has grown," I noted. Not that it rivaled in any way Arierona's great house. Wings had been added on either end, and porches. This was an abode that could receive guests.

Teme stood on the front porch, tall, and lean as ever, her husband beside her. Her eyes swept across our party. "There is room for all of you," she announced. "Will you stay in the king's house, Taona?" she asked. "I know he keeps a chamber ready for you."

Marareta's tone remained polite, almost formal. "But I have family with me this time, Lady Teme. If you have the space, my wife and son will stay here with me." I think most of us knew that if he shared that other room, it would be with Pana'a. Certainly Panoha did.

What of Ma'ave? If any friction existed between her and Teme, neither made it known. They embraced and then my best friend turned to me. "Rahiniti," was all she sighed as she wrapped her long arms around me. "I missed you."

And I had missed her. Maybe I would never leave! She stepped back and took a look at both me and Ma'ave. "You two do not mind sharing a chamber, do you? And your little one, Lady Ma'ave."

"Probably Malee, as well," I said. "I do not think we will be too crowded."

Ma'ave bowed her head graciously. "I will gladly share with Rahiniti and I gladly accept your hospitality." Then she chuckled and said in a loud aside to me, "Even were Teme and I still rivals, I would rather not share a house with Iro."

"Maybe Iro is hoping to make amends for his past mistakes," said Bafa, as all followed our host into his house.

"Some pretty big mistakes, as I remember it," remarked Gordie.

Ma'ave laughed at that, maybe louder than was necessary. "Iro is a little like you, Lord Gordie, in that he is good at convincing people to see things his way. Except his way is often the wrong one! He also is genuine in his politics, a true Owl."

Owls was the name given to the party of the traditionalists. Originally an insult, they now wore it like a tattoo, to proclaim who they were.

"And what of your politics, Ma'ave?" he replied.

"I have, ah, distanced myself from the traditionalists. I —" She seemed a bit abashed, but continued. "I favored that faction mostly because Ikataki had taken leadership among the Parrots."

"And now he is thoroughly disgraced, there is room for you!"

laughed Teme. "Come and eat. There is a lunch spread for everyone. Yes, all you who serve and guard, too."

"I am sure Arierona will feast you tomorrow," added Bafa. "You'll have to make do with what we steal from him today."

Teme punched him on the arm, as he certainly deserved. "Did Aranu already leave?" she then asked, looking about. "No matter. I expect he and Amirea will show up here later."

Being an informal lunch — and the house of the more-than-informal Bafa — the children remained with us, though they ate at a separate mat. There seemed an unvoiced agreement to allow Marareta and Panoha the highest places at our own mat. We nobles were still clustered around Teme and Bafa.

"It is a fine house, Lord Bafa," spoke Toare. "Do you then intend to remain here?" Although he was the adopted son of Arierona, Bafa would have no claim on his kingdom, nor, for that matter, on any other property in the Mora homeland. Teme had little in the way of an inheritance due her, as well, though as sister to Poneiva, she could remain in his house or have one bestowed upon her. Even the one in which Ma'ave and Pua now resided.

"Ponu has said he wishes me to stay," answered Bafa. "When and if the kingship passes to him."

"May that be long yet," murmured Marareta, between mouthfuls of baked yam.

"Indeed," agreed Bafa. "Ponu appreciates my contributions to the kingdom, I think." He winked at Teme. "Almost as much as he likes having the sister of the High King living here."

"He only likes having the three best archers in all the Mora lands at his call," she responded. "But tell them of his offer."

"Well," began Bafa, "you know I am interested in the rocks in the hills and along the coast."

"Too interested," I could not help remarking. Teme managed to stifle her laugh.

Bafa ignored me. "The land out that way is largely empty.

Ponu and Arierona have brought up the idea of me setting up a household there, being a noble vassal like Teme's father." He turned to his wife. "Or *to* Teme's father. It might be argued that area is part of his holdings."

"It's not very good land," noted Marareta.

"There's worse. And I could keep an eye on the hills, and the Salt Coast beyond."

"If it's hills and empty land you want," said Gordie, "there's plenty enough of both in the opposite direction."

"We know," Teme said. "We saw enough of them last year." She put an arm around her husband's shoulders. "I think we should stick closer to home."

Gordie shrugged. "Someone will want to take possession there someday. And neither I nor the High King may be able to stop them."

Ma'ave nodded. "It is of such things we must speak, Lord Gordie, you and I, you and Poneiva."

"But not now," said Bafa. "It's getting close to time for an afternoon nap."

And that was proof that Bafa can sometimes be quite sensible.

40. From the Lake

"OF COURSE, I *am* interested in the land Gordie mentioned," said Bafa. "There are veins of copper in those hills, waiting for me to come and free them."

"It would be hard to do it unnoticed," was Marareta's thought. "You have found tin on the coasts here, haven't you?"

"Bits of the crystalline ore," was the answer. "Not a real source yet."

None of this did I much understand. Nor did I understand why men would speak of such things beside the beauty that is A'auwa. Toare was the only who seemed to be giving the lake the reverence it deserved.

Ah, Lugan stood again in the skies of dawn. Or I should say Rehe, shouldn't I? If I am Mora, I must have Mora gods.

Which made me think of something else. "I must go across the lake to visit Hito." I turned to Toare. "And your mother."

"They'll come here if we wait," he replied. "I think we'll all be too busy today anyway."

"We?" Bafa laughed outright. "Everyone will be busy but you!"

The boy looked offended. "Ponu asked me to sing after the feast tonight," he informed us.

"And if we are to be the guests of honor at that feast we'd best not wander to the far side of A'auwa," said Marareta. "Later, perhaps, I might like to visit there myself."

"Gordie should definitely go," I added.

He nodded absentmindedly, scanning the mists above the dark water. "A canoe comes."

Before the sun was risen, Marareta had chosen to walk beside A'auwa. Now I knew why. Bafa and I, early risers, had followed along — I simply because I liked the idea of visiting the lake. Bafa perhaps hoped to have words with the taona, without others vying for the man's attention.

Toare? I had grabbed the sleepy boy when he shuffled out

onto the porch, seeking breakfast. "You were right," I whispered to him. "Your mother and Hito came on their own." Two women wielded paddles behind them, priestesses of the isle.

Neither was Pana'a. Marareta showed none of the disappointment I am sure he felt. He stepped forward in greeting.

The priestesses pulled their craft onto the sandy shore. "Pana'a will come later, Taona," called one. "We brought these two in her stead." With that, they were away to the House of Arierona, on some business of their own.

I let the others greet the couple first, watched Toare embrace his mother and then Hito — a man he could call 'father,' though I much doubted he ever would.

The man who had brought me out of the realms of the Kohari, my homeland, and started me on the path to being Rahiniti, Mora noblewoman. The man who was my first lover. Much I owed Hito and much I cared for him still.

But I could not share his life. I think we had both known that when we parted at the House of Marareta, years ago, I to become daughter to Temani'itu, he to search for his direction as a priest. Now, seeing him here, at last at peace, there was no longer any question. I must look elsewhere for my path and maybe it was a way walked by Gordie.

No time to mull on that now. I stepped forward and greeted the Lady Mehetu and Hito — should he be called 'Master' now, as the old priest Hoka was before him? I certainly was not going to refer to him as 'lord,' even if marrying a noblewoman did entitle him to it!

"Let's feed you two," spoke Bafa. "Or allow Arierona to do so. Some of our guests may be seeking breakfast by now."

Marareta chuckled. "And you don't object to having a second one."

Toare and I fell in at the rear. "I like Hito," he told me,

150

keeping his voice low. "I always have, and was happy to see him marry my mother."

"I think he has found that he sought," I replied. "Would we all might."

"It would help if I knew what that was," said the young man, and no more for a time. Then, slowly, an afterthought. "At least I found my path as a bard."

"Yet you trained as a warrior."

"It was to honor my father, and his wishes, that I persisted with learning the ways of the warrior in the House of Anana. I was at the age to do so when he was slain."

"It was never truly what you wished, was it?" I asked.

"Perhaps a part of me did." A shrug, followed by a laugh. "Perhaps part still does."

This I could understand. A part of me still longed to dance, as I had been trained most of my life. Were I yet in the temple, I might be teaching by now. Or, married and elsewhere; one never knew when one of the dancers might catch the eye of some noble or high-ranking priest. But I, too, had chosen another path.

Untypical of noble houses, Arierona's 'eating porch' was on the corner of his home, not on the side. The southwest corner it was, or more southwest than any other direction. I thought it a sensible arrangement, an integral part of the house's structure yet open on two sides to let the breeze through. We climbed the dark, well-worn wooden steps; it was still early and few were at breakfast here.

"None of our visitors are hungry yet, it seems," spoke Mehetu. She squinted into the shadows. "Is that someone waving to us?"

"Ponu," said Bafa. "Let us join him."

That the king's second had hoped for this meeting, I suspected. Ponu probably did not need my counsel but I filled a bowl and joined the rest.

"Your words too I wish to hear, Master Hito," the stocky

nobleman was saying as I took a place. The highest place for I somewhat outranked Mehetu. No men of Ponu sat with us, though an attendant knelt behind his master.

"I am but a priest," came his objection.

"One might say the same of the Taona Marareta." He looked from the one man to the other, peering from beneath thick eyebrows. "Both also warriors, and the most practical of priests."

Marareta smiled the slightest of smiles. "Practical men do not go off across the mountains."

"Unless forced," added Hito. "We neither truly had a choice, Taona."

"There is always a choice," came Marareta's reply. "But speak to us, Lord Ponu." He turned his seeming attention to the peeling of an orange as the nobleman began.

"My words are of Iro," began Ponu. "His arrival here was unexpected."

"By his former wife, too," I had to say.

"Yes. We had ample warning of her coming. As an emissary of the High King, I understand?"

He was unsure about the woman, then. Perhaps that, as much as any other reason, was why he met with us. "Unofficially," Marareta told him. "To carry back her thoughts to Poneiva."

Ponu nodded, slowly, thoughtfully. Or he looked thoughtful, anyway. "With the loss of Ma'ave, his status has lessened, but he remains a voice among the traditionalists."

"And they have concerns?" asked Bafa.

"Iro does raise questions about our visitor from the north." The man sighed. "I think it would be best to allow him in any councils we may hold."

"Some of them," spoke Hito. "Not necessarily all."

To which Marareta gave firm agreement and turned his attention again to his breakfast.

41. Iro

"That he plotted against the High King, I have figured out. And I unwittingly helped him in some of that!"

Marareta considered Iro's words. "Do you think he plots again? That he might be one who would do harm to Lord Gordie?"

The little man shook his head vigorously. "There would be no advantage in it for him. But," he confided, "he has told me that some approached him. Ikataki wanted nothing to do with them." Iro slightly arched one eyebrow. "Or so he claimed."

"His claims mean little," stated Ma'ave, flatly. "We both know that." I think she had completely missed the subtle — but sharp — edge on Iro's words. The Lady Ma'ave was not subtle at all, was she? All business.

It was no wonder they parted. Oh, yes, yes, I know there was more to it. But here both were, in the central room of the House of Bafa. Here we all were. It was crowded, for Bafa's home is not so large!

Marareta decided it best Ti'ine not attend this council — and all deferred to the taona — for Iro would surely carry tales of him back. Back to whom? We were uncertain. Nor was Toare there, off practicing for his performance later. Not that the boy would have added anything.

Oh, truly, neither would I. Perhaps I should have been elsewhere too, maybe with Pahe, watching over the children.

"So who approached Ikataki?" wondered Bafa. "Did he say?"

"Only that they were nobles of the northern kingdoms, concerned about Lord Gordie's growing power across the hills." Iro lowered his voice just the least, as if imparting a secret. "I got the impression King Naire might give their cause some support."

Bafa frowned at this. "That doesn't sound like Naire at all. He is not one to upset the order of things."

"My husband is fond of the old man," spoke Teme. "We both

owe him our gratitude, as well, for coming to our aid at the House of Momana."

That Bafa also wanted to find his precious rocks in the hills that border Naire's realm might have played a part. But not all here knew of those. Ah, I was keeping a secret from Gordie, wasn't I? That was not a good thing, I was fairly sure!

"One reason I am here is to deal with those concerns," said Gordie. "The more I know of such things, the better, when I speak again with Poneiva."

Now those were the sort of words we wanted Iro to carry back to his fellow Owls. I noted again the expression of approval on the face of Ma'ave, as I had when they first met in the House of Marareta.

"Perhaps I might meet some of those nobles when I make my way back to the House of the High King," Gordie continued. "I shall be making my way across country rather than back down the river." A subtle invitation. Even I could see that was well done.

There was going to be no more discussion of substance. That, too, I could see. We snacked on the fresh fruits of Areirona's gardens and gossiped of little things for a time. It was hours yet to the evening feast. Time enough for a nap.

And then to tend to the children before heading to the House of Arierona. Malee could not understand why she was not allowed to attend; Mora ways did not always make sense to her. Nor to me, for that matter.

"You must wait until you have breasts," Maratoa informed her. "Tita wasn't allowed to eat with the grownups until she did."

"Then you shouldn't until yours grow too," was her rather sensible reply.

Fortunately, I did have breasts — and quite nice ones if I say so myself — and was soon accompanying my friends through the gardens of Arierona, beneath arching fruit trees and hibiscus nearly as large. This meal would be no great feast, only a gathering in the king's central room, we and a few nobles in attendance.

And Pana'a, come from her sacred isle. She took a seat to my left, though I think her rank as High Priestess would have let her claim pretty much any spot she chose. Gordie, of course, was at the right hand of Arierona, as befitted a visiting king — a king in all but name.

Directly to his right, Marareta, with Panoha accorded a similar position among the women. This, I understood — the taona's lost wife, Rahaita, was the daughter of the king. He would always sit high at the feasts of Arierona.

"I have felt the presence of the children," spoke Pana'a, with no other introduction. "Were Malee Mora born, we would ask that she come to our isle to be trained in prophesy."

"Gordie would never agree to it, Mora or not," I replied. Of that I was more than certain. "The shaman Oorto is training her. Maratoa, too." Her son.

The priestess nodded. Of course she knew this. Had she spoken to Marareta? I knew he was too dutiful to be with her when his wife was here. That was his nature. The taona took such things seriously.

"We must speak on the morrow," Pana'a said. "You and I and the other women, maybe. Of many things we must speak. But tonight, let us fill our stomachs and think of nothing more!"

Excellent advice, I felt, and so I took it. Then while the men — oh, and more than some of the women — turned to the talk of politics, I slipped away from the House of Arierona. Down to the shores of A'auwa I went, to converse with the lake. Perhaps she had some wisdom for me.

For I time I walked the shore, beneath the dark pines. The clouds that brought afternoon rains were melting away, leaving a vault of sparkling jewels above. Someone joined me, a man, to my left. Short, for a Mora. Iro.

"Might I walk with you, Lady Rahiniti?" he asked.

I but nodded. The nobleman fell in beside me, keeping his silence for a while. "The Lady Teme is your friend," he said eventually. Whether it was a statement or a question, I was uncertain.

"She is," I replied. The best friend I had.

"She holds me in low regard." His chuckle suggested a mild self-mockery. I suspected it was assumed. "Even lower than my former wife."

"Doesn't she have reason, Lord Iro?" I asked. How could I not? Yet I knew things were not so simple — they never are. "But she does not understand the ways of politics, I think. Not really." I was not sure even Ma'ave did, truly.

"What I do now is important, I believe. Smoothing things. I am neither a warrior nor a wise counselor, my lady, I am aware. But this," Iro stated, "is what I am good at."

"Carrying words between those who might misunderstand each other, were they speaking face to face," I said. He looked on me with some surprise.

I laughed. "I grew up with the intrigues of the Temple of Mihasa, my lord," I informed him. "I can see things." That and dancing was all I had learned there!

"Ah, I would have done better to marry you, maybe!" He laughed at the suggestion and I joined him. Images of very short children flitted through my mind. Maybe he was serious, at least a bit; I am still not sure.

There was never another opportunity to find out. Two figures rushed from the cover of the trees. One careened into me, knocking me to the needle-covered ground, and all the breath from me. Knives flashed. Iro crumpled.

42. Hearing and Telling

"IT COULD HAVE been mistaken identity," felt Aranu. "They might have thought Lord Gordie walked with the lady."

Ponu considered this. "It is possible. What other reason would they have for slaying this man?"

I had to speak. "Because he would pass along counsel friendly to Gordie. Just meeting with him was probably enough."

The third nobleman there, Toare, caught onto this at once. "Gordie's enemies wish to prevent any sort of agreement between him and the Mora."

I had sat and shaken for some time after the assassins had disappeared, unable to catch a breath and raise an alarm. At last I had risen and called to a passing pair of warriors. Word swiftly reached the king and his second.

"So they hope to create dissension," said Ponu. "That sounds likely, Lady Rahiniti. Ho, you, bring that torch closer." He regarded the fallen Iro for a few seconds and shook his head. "Bear him back to the king's house," he ordered. "Someone must inform the Lady Ma'ave."

I think he felt that duty was his, but it was one he did not relish. "I can do it, Lord Ponu," spoke Toare. He glanced toward me, clearly hoping for my help in this.

"We might do well to inform others first," I told him. Not that I thought we needed help in this task; Ma'ave would take the news well enough. But for her daughter, little Aeta, I ached.

"Marareta sits with the king," said Aranu. "He already knows."

I had no idea whom we should seek out first as we turned to the house. Bafa, perhaps? Or even Teme — there seemed an odd bond between her and Ma'ave these days. Not friendship, but a mutual respect.

"Ma'ave joked with me about losing a spouse," I told Toare, as we made our way up the long slope toward the House of Arierona. "Now that has grown serious."

He nodded solemnly, and turned his eyes to an approaching figure, silhouetted against the torches that burnt before the house. "It is Ma'ave," he said.

She spoke without any greeting. "Is it so?" the noblewoman asked. "Gossip spreads quickly and servants are whispering all through the king's house."

"It is. Iro lies dead." Best to just say it. "Two men attacked him as we walked beside the water."

Ma'ave sighed deeply. "The man could not keep out of trouble." She turned back the way she had come, walking with us in silence to the House of Bafa. "I must see to Aeta," she said as we mounted the front steps.

No more did we see of her that night. Most of the others who guested in that house, however, were gathered in the common room, waiting for our words. This, I left mostly to Toare; it is his trade, after all.

"Ma'ave still cared for the man who was her husband," he said as he finished up. "That can be seen. That I did see when I stayed in the House of Pua."

Bafa spoke. "I believe your assessment of the reasons for this murder are right, Toare."

"Rahiniti's assessment," the boy corrected him. I could see both Gordie and Pahe nod knowingly at this.

And Bafa knew me rather well himself. "That doesn't surprise me." He looked to Gordie. "Those men would surely target you if you went strolling by A'auwa. And they are still out there somewhere."

More like them too, maybe, I thought. Had they known who I was, they might have attempted to take me. I could be used against Gordie. "No one should walk alone," I said.

"And we must post guards here," added Pahe. "More guards."

Bafa nodded. "Best you all remain in my house, rather than being scattered." There was no more to be said then, so we went our ways. My way was to my sleeping chamber. Malee and Aeta both slumbered there, and Ma'ave beside them. Soon, I did as well.

The little girls were quietly playing together when my eyes again opened. Ma'ave? Gone. It was unusual for her to rise before me.

"Have you eaten yet?" I asked. Malee shook her head. "Come, then. Let's go find some of Lord Bafa's food." I noted a guard stood outside our room as we exited, one of Gordie's men. He followed us down the narrow hall. Pahe's orders, no doubt.

Aeta's mother sat on the porch, in conversation with Gordie and the Kohari messenger Ti'ine. I had no desire to share in whatever intrigues they discussed so I took the girls and our filled bowls to another mat. We were shortly joined by Panoha and little Rahiri.

The woman took a long look at Aeta, before addressing me. "Does she know?"

"I do not think so."

Panoha methodically broke up coconut meat to dole out to the young ones. "It is for her mother to tell her, but with the gossip flying about Arierona's compound, she is bound to hear." Her eyes now were on Malee, not Ma'ave's daughter.

Yes, Malee, would be more likely to learn of Iro's death and speak of it to her friend. Older, and a bright girl, she was. I should say something to her when we were alone. She would understand. Too well, she would understand.

"Maratoa is not with us this morning?" I asked, feeling it best not to dwell on the subject of death.

"With Oorto and his father," came Panoha's reply. "In the House of Arierona." Her smile held a trace of sadness. "The old king wants to see his grandson."

"Hmm. He, too, might hear, ah, things."

"Marareta will make certain he knows not to speak of them."

But boys are forgetful and impetuous. Oh, certainly, girls can be too! Ma'ave had best not take too long before speaking to her daughter.

I glimpsed someone approaching from the corner of my eye — Ma'ave herself. Her companions stood, seeming to wait on her, where they had breakfasted. "I greet you, my ladies," she said. "Aeta, you and I are going to go for a walk. And you too, Malee. Your father and Ti'ine will come with us."

The two girls scrambled to their feet and ran to Gordie. "I shall have help in this, I hope," stated Ma'ave, and nodded a goodbye to us. In a few moments, all five had disappeared into the house.

"It is odd," remarked Panoha, pulling her little daughter onto her lap, "that they did not include you in this."

Perhaps it was. Ti'ine was probably included as a bodyguard. Nothing strange there. Gordie and Malee were two who had known recent loss, two who understood in their own and different ways.

And I? I didn't seem to be of much use to anyone.

43. Pana'a

"You were with Demba?" asked Amirea.

"I was," I replied. "I or Gordie was always at her side until — until the end." Suddenly, all the emotions of that time rushed back upon me and tears began. "Oh, I'm sorry," I sobbed.

"Don't be," she said, embracing me. Why, she was crying as much as I. And why not? Demba was her best friend, the friend she had made as a stranger in a new world, though they had seen little of each other in recent times.

"It was good that I was able to visit this year past," she said, sitting back again and wiping the tears from her eyes. Then she asked, quite unexpectedly, "Are you going to marry Gordie?"

How had she heard of that? Oh, no sense in asking. Among Gordie's men were those who would gossip of such things. Not the closed-mouth Pahe, of course, but others. Perhaps the rumor had reached Aranu's ears; he would be eager to repeat it to his wife.

"I do not know," was my answer, as it had been before. "He did ask." It was the first time I had actually said that to anyone.

"You do not love him."

"I suppose not." I hadn't even been spending much time with the man.

"You don't have to marry at all, you know," said Amirea. "Take a new lover each season!" She giggled. "I would not even have thought of such a thing before coming to this land, much less suggested it."

I remembered women like that in the Temple of Mihasa, freed of any obligations of being a wife. It was not a life I had coveted but one I might have ended up living.

"Pana'a and her priestesses do not marry," I observed. "I was supposed to meet with her this morning but —" I shrugged. Everyone's plans had changed since last night's events.

"Let's go find her," suggested my companion. Amirea seemed to think nothing of leaving her children with their nurses and doing as she wished. In this, she was not unlike other Mora noblewomen, though she had been born in another world. Maybe noblewomen there were the same.

Could that be why I was considering Gordie's proposal? I did not wish to abandon Malee. And was this a good enough reason? It was something I must think upon further. "Very well," I said. "I have no idea where she might be."

But Pana'a was not hard to find. As we passed out onto Arierona's front porch, there she sat with Teme. Waiting for us? "Let us go to A'auwa," she suggested. Or perhaps she ordered it. No matter. We went, with a pair of burly warriors to serve as guards.

"I will paddle back to my island this evening," the priestess told us. "Hito has already returned across A'auwa to his shrine of Teva. You must visit him there, Rahiniti. You and all your friends."

"I hope to." If I could persuade Gordie.

"It is of Malee and Maratoa I wished to speak. Mostly of Malee and Maratoa."

"Should that not be a discussion for their fathers?" asked Teme.

"I have spoken with Oorto of their education," she replied. "He can better explain that to Gordie and Marareta." We had reached the shore and Pana'a spent a moment gazing out over the lake, glass-like on this still midmorn, before turning to me. "He tells me Malee may remain in the House of Marareta for a time — and that you may remain with her."

Again? "It is possible."

"She will need someone, with both her parents gone. Marareta would welcome your presence, whatever your status might be."

That was surely true. Yet what concern of mine would any of it be if I were not married to Gordie, if I did not become Malee's mother? I answered, "I had thought maybe to remain here. There is no place I better love." My eyes went to Teme. "And here live my friends."

All this was true. I had no desire, certainly, to go live in the House of Gordie, now that I had returned to the shores of A'auwa. I had said it finally, made words of my thoughts, and better understood them.

Teme and Amirea both had their own thoughts as they regarded me without speaking; Pana'a, however, was looking somewhere beyond me. "Whether you choose to be with your Malee or not, she comes to see you now." I turned to see Ma'ave approaching with the two little girls, a trio of warriors guarding them.

Malee ran to me, embraced me. Then she looked up with curiosity at the tall priestess.

"This is Pana'a," I told her.

"Like the falls?" she asked. Without waiting for an answer she posed another question. "Are we going to go see them?" I had promised, after all.

"Your father has decided it is too dangerous," spoke Ma'ave.

I do not know if Malee or I was the more disappointed. But there was a more important question at the moment than whether we might go see the Pool of the Moon and the high falls that plunged to it. "Aeta?" I asked. I need say no more than that.

"Yes, though I am not certain how much she understands." She looked to the pair of girls, now holding hands and gazing out at the wide lake. "Malee helped me in this. She is wise for one so little."

I, too, looked upon the two for a moment. "It is good to have a friend in such times."

"In any times," said Teme.

To that, we were all in agreement.

44. Mothers

"I WANT TO go out to the island," declared Malee. She stood looking in the proper direction, but it could not be seen from Arierona's corner porch.

"You must be invited," Mehetu told her, when neither I nor Teme seemed to know how to respond to this. Hito's wife had remained in the House of Arierona when the priest departed — to spend time with her son, I assumed. Where that son was, I had no idea.

"They might keep you there," warned Maratoa. "Make you a priestess and never let you come back again!"

The girl might have half-believed him. "Pana'a wouldn't do that." She frowned. "You 'ave two mommies and I don't 'ave any. Can I 'ave one of them?"

The boy had a ready answer. "Rahiniti can be your mother." Even he knew about this!

She peered at me a moment, almost as if she were appraising me. "No," she decided, "I think I want Ma-vay as my mommy. Then Aeta could 'ave a daddy."

And she and Aeta would be sisters. But it was a ridiculous idea — Gordie husband to Ma'ave? Ha, I could imagine what Pahe would think of that!

Mehetu changed the subject, for which I was more than grateful. I think she knew this. "Toare's master is on the way here. A messenger this morning puts him but a couple days away."

Teme, half-asleep, was roused by the news. "Ulani comes?"

"Yes, and your brother Beka, and Mouiri."

"Mouiri?" She seemed confused by that.

"He now serves Beka," I told her. "I think he is grooming him to take over as admiral."

She laughed. "Poneiva's idea, no doubt. Or even Ulani's."

"And perhaps first suggested to one of them by Lady Pua,"

added Mehetu. It would not be surprising, as she was mother of both Ulani and Mouiri.

"This will mean another round of councils and meetings," I realized. "And then, perhaps, Gordie will wish to leave A'auwa."

"You have not decided yet whether to leave with him," said Teme. Immediately, she regretted this, for Malee turned to stare at me.

It would be best to speak honestly. "I shall accompany Lord Gordie as far as the House of the High King," I announced. "Beyond that, after that, I do not know. Not yet." This had always been my intention, truly. I would not really have remained here — but I might well return.

And whether Malee would remain in the House of Marareta was still not certain. If so, I decided right then, I would accompany her. But beyond that, again, I had no plan.

Suddenly, I felt I wanted to talk with Hito and ask his advice. He had guided me to this land and to this life. Who better to help me now?

"Your husband left too soon," I complained to Mehetu. "I barely saw him."

"He is not so far away," she reminded me. "You could paddle across A'auwa and visit him anytime."

"And take me to the island," added Malee. She was not going to forget that.

"You *feel* the island, don't you?" I asked. The girl had said something of the sort when we first stood by A'auwa.

She only nodded, but Maratoa was bursting to tell us what he knew. "Oorto says the walls between the worlds are thinner there. That makes it easier to see things that are going to happen."

"It also lets through the dreams that drive some mad. That was the fate of Pana'a's sister," said Teme. "The wife of Arierona and mother of Rahaita." Her own eyes turned toward the hidden isle. "This is not a safe place for those with such gifts."

"Rahaita was my mother," said Maratoa. "One of them."

"You know, though, who your birth mother is," said Mehetu.

"Uh-huh. Pana'a."

"King Hara'a, he who slew Rahaita, was another driven to madness by his gifts," Teme said. "He, too, could feel the presence of the island."

"You killed him," said the boy. "You're in an epic!"

"It is so," Teme admitted.

He tilted his head and gave her a long look. "Could you teach me to shoot the bow, Lady Teme?"

"Gladly, Noble Maratoa," she replied. "How else might you become the greatest of warriors?" Teme, of a sudden, grinned broadly. "Or perhaps the second greatest." I gave her a puzzled look. I suspect Mehetu did as well.

"This is as good a time as any to tell you," Teme said, "but let it go no further for now." She leaned in and whispered, "I am with child."

"Pana'a's prophecy names your son as a future High King," said Mehetu, almost as quietly.

"Whether this will be that son or another, or perhaps a daughter, only the gods know," spoke Teme. "If it is a boy, we shall name him Maneata, after my slain brother."

I knew the name. How? Ah, he was killed during the raid that burnt the Temple of Mihasa. Yes, I had heard that epic more than once! It was Beka's courage in protecting Maneata and bearing the body back to the Mora canoes that led Poneiva to name him brother.

"The perfect choice," I told her. But I am sure she already knew it.

45. Brothers

"I NEVER GOT the chance to sing at Arierona's feast," Toare complained. "The news of Iro came as I sat with the king, and Aranu and Ponu and I rushed off." He lifted his eyes briefly to my face. "I was worried about you."

"There will be other feasts," I said. Silly boy.

"With Ulani here, I won't be asked. It was my chance to make a mark."

"Ah, and it is all my fault you were prevented!"

He laughed at the absurdity of that. "Indeed, Rahiniti. You have ruined my career."

"I thought you were capable of doing that yourself," I told him. "Are there any more mulberries? No, not the sapa. They're not as good."

He shrugged and started to put the sapa fruit back into his bowl. On second thought, he popped it into his own mouth. "Both bland," Toare said. "Is Kohari food better?"

"We live on kuru," I stated. "Boiled." There was little in the world that is more bland than kuru fruit. Hito had a great hatred for it, having consumed too much as an impoverished boy.

"I hope Teme's family grows more coffee trees," he said. "I liked what I tried."

I had not been impressed. There was no need to say so. "Maybe she and Bafa will plant some if they set up a household in the empty lands." I had no idea if it was good land for coffee. I don't think anyone did. Not anyone Mora.

"Even so, it will take years to grow enough. What's the tumult over there?"

I looked to the knot of men and women gathered by the way into the house. "News about something?" I hazarded, and rose from my place. "Let's find out." We had dawdled long enough on Arierona's porch.

One of the women, a servant in the house, spied our approach and rushed to us. Or to Toare, I should say. "Master Toare," she gasped, "it is the Taona Ulani! He was attacked on the road here." A pause to gather herself, a gulp of air. "Some say he was slain." This last, almost a whisper.

Normally, Toare would have objected to the use of 'master' before his name, nor was the bard Ulani customarily styled 'taona,' but this was no time for such quibbles! "I thank you for this news," was his grave acknowledgment of her words. To me, he said, "There will surely be warriors on the way north. I must join them." With that he hurried into the house.

It was to be expected the boy would be concerned about his master. I wished that I might join him and those warriors, but none would want the silly little woman Rahiniti along. If only for my short legs would slow them down! Best I go to the House of Bafa, give this news there, and wait.

Through the day we waited, each of us in our own way. Marareta and Bafa at once went to the House of Arierona; whether they accompanied those who went north, I did not know. Oorto turned his attention to the children, showing no concern, though I knew he cared about Ulani. Most of the rest of us sat on Bafa's porch, saying little.

"I wish Ma'ave would stop fidgeting," Teme whispered to me. The woman did a great deal of getting up, sitting down, moving from room to room. But she had two brothers to worry about, for both Ulani and Mouiri had been among those attacked.

And I? I was fond of Ulani but not close to him. My thoughts turned, rather, to Toare, rushing north to his master's side. Might all danger be passed, I prayed — to Rehe I prayed but maybe I addressed her as Lugan once or twice.

Near dusk, a man, one of those who served the king, came and spoke privately to Teme. "The first report has come," she announced when she had heard his news, "from a messenger who ran back south to the House of Arierona. They are coming, walking through the night, carrying the wounded."

"What of Ulani?" came Ma'ave's question. She spoke carefully, keeping her emotions under control.

"He numbered among those hurt. That is all we know." Teme's eyes swept across those gathered. "We shall eat. Then I intend to wait at the House of Arierona."

Most nodded or murmured agreement with that proposition, I among them. I could not help smiling at Teme taking charge; not so different from her brother the High King was she at times.

Was it a burden to her, being a high noble? I was not sure I could fill such a role, although I, too, was *ari noe* by adoption, and I might one day rule in the House of Gordie. Ah, perhaps I could do it well enough but knew I did not desire it.

With a crowd of others, we sat on or near the front porch of the king's house, watching, by the light of torch and oil lamp, of stars and a half-full moon. One could glimpse, now and then, a glint of their reflection on A'auwa, through the trees that rose tall and black beside the lake. "Lights!" cried someone. Yes, distant, points of flame along the roadway south, growing closer as the minutes passed.

Some carried torches down to the road and waited there; I ached to join them but remembered the dangers of separating from those who guarded me, who guarded Gordie. Gordie? Where was he? I was not sure he had even accompanied us. Maybe he felt it better to remain close to his daughter.

Ponu came out onto the porch, and Arierona, too, borne in a litter. His nephew helped him out and stood close beside the king. The son of Arierona's sister, Ponu was; that I knew, but little more. The two looked much alike, stocky, with thick, dark eyebrows that met in the middle.

Now the torches were close and turned to move toward the house. There was Aranu at their head. He must have led those who

169

went south. Where was Toare? There, beside one of the litters. No need to guess who was being carried.

Aranu stopped at the bottom of the steps to report to his king. One of Arierona's highest captains he had become, a captain of captains, and one trusted to carry out such missions as these. He had trained as a warrior in this house, far from the realm of his father, King Hei'iro, and had once been a suitor of Rahaita. Yes, I had heard all these tales from my friends. Mora are great tellers of stories, both gossip and epic poems.

"I return with your guests, my lord," he announced. "Two we bear are dead, and some wounded. Best these be attended to."

"Let it be so," said the king. A nod from Ponu sent men forward. "I give you the welcome of the House of Arierona, travelers." The man swayed a little on his feet, to be steadied by his attendants. He shrugged them off, a bit peevishly I thought, and asked, "Lord Beka is here?"

"I am, my lord," said the big man, stepping forward. Mouiri was at his side, one arm in a sling. His left. "I fear Master Ulani is seriously hurt. A large group of warriors attacked us where the road climbs near Pana'a."

There was no mistaking the anger on the face of Arierona. "Such should not happen in my kingdom." He turned to Ponu. "We will speak of it in the morning." I would not have wanted to be Ponu right then. Even less so in the morning.

Ponu and the attendants helped the king into his litter and all disappeared into the house. By now, the wounded were also being helped in. Teme stepped forward and stopped a warrior she seemed to know — one of her brother's men, I guessed. "How fares Master Ulani?" she asked of him.

"He took several wounds, my lady," the man replied. "We do not think them fatal." He sounded somewhat uncertain. "The attackers outnumbered us. Lord Beka expected no trouble on this journey!"

"Nor did anyone else." Teme turned to Ma'ave — she and I flanked the noblewoman — saying, "Ulani was surely the target."

"I do not think they expected Beka and Mouiri to be with him," the warrior said. "I doubt he would live had they not been. They are potent warriors."

"Our brothers," spoke Ma'ave, managing a weak smile. "We are fortunate to have them."

Part IV. The Morning Star

46. Ulani

"I mourn for Ri'i," said Ulani, pushing himself to a seated position. "I should have sent him home."

"It was his choice, Master," Toare reminded him.

"So it was, yet I *shall* mourn. That is only right." He held his silence for a moment. "Two battles on the road, one for each of us," mused the bard. "We should each craft a poem and present them as a pair."

"Mine would be most brief. There were but three attackers, and Marareta slew two of them."

"You could always make up some extra assailants," I told him. The boy looked scandalized but Ulani laughed.

"We faced a dozen who burst out of ambush." He winked at me. "Maybe more!"

"Against eight well-trained warriors," Toare pointed out. "One of them a hero."

"True," Ulani admitted. "But those who attacked were warriors, as well. I can recognize that. I saw enough untrained rabble during the civil war to know the difference." He gazed into space, remembering, perhaps, before going on. "Four we left dead before the rest ran, taking their wounded with them."

I could not help but smile a little at his 'we.' Ulani was no warrior. "You should rest," I said. "Much blood was lost."

"And my leg aches dreadfully," announced the bard. "Is there any wine in this house? Or even beer?"

"I shall search all the House of Bafa, Master," promised Toare, "and that of Arierona, if need be."

"That is well," spoke Ulani, stretching again on his mat. In a few moments, he slept.

Most of Ulani's wounds were not so serious, cuts and bruises, but a spear had gone through his right thigh. It was badly hurt; Ulani might be lame the rest of his life. He would certainly limp.

"It will be days before Ulani has strength enough to move about. Maybe weeks," stated Toare, as we left the room.

I nodded. This I knew. "Gordie says we shall remain until we know he is well."

"And he can speak politics with him?"

"Maybe. But I think he does this mostly at the request of Lady Ma'ave."

"I have had a request of another noblewoman," he said. "My mother. She wishes to cross A'auwa to her husband and asks that I accompany her." A pause. "Would you care to come along?"

A better way than most to fill up a day. "Oorto might want to come too."

"Oh, to visit Ruiru. I am surprised he hasn't gone over there already. Or Ruiru hasn't come here."

We had walked as far as Bafa's south porch. "Maybe our entire group would like to visit the shrines. We should ask."

At this, Toare made a sour face. I think he had seen too much of them. "Or not," I laughed. "But definitely Oorto."

"Maybe some warriors, too?" he wondered. "To guard you?"

It was a good question. "No one will know I am going," I decided, "even if they cared. Let's not attract attention by taking men with us." I did not know if I would be any sort of target.

"Someone might think to use you against Gordie," said Toare.

"I think they would be mistaken." Did I really? Would Gordie care enough?

He squinted at me but said no more of it. As long as we were on the porch, we filled food bowls and took a place on the floor. It was close enough to lunchtime, and Ulani's wine could wait.

"I do think we understand why Ulani was attacked," Toare said, after a time. "The same reason as Iro."

"To impede an understanding between Gordie and the Mora," I answered. "Ha, our betters are probably discussing this very thing elsewhere."

"Marareta and Bafa and Gordie?" he asked.

"Beka and Ma'ave too, I would suspect. And Teme would never allow herself to be left out." I gazed out at the collection of huts and small garden patches beyond the House of Bafa. "We two are a bit useless. It will be good to go see Hito tomorrow."

"When Ulani is better, there will be more discussion. He has the High King's ear."

"Until then, someone might actually ask you to sing."

"This is so," he admitted. "Maybe I shall compose the poem he suggested, that of our journey here." A momentary frown. "Most of it is not very exciting."

"What of your rescue of Malee?" I asked. "Not many bards get to sing of their own deeds."

The boy raised an eyebrow at me. "With good reason, I would think. We would be far too inclined to embellish. Hmm, I think instead I shall get all the tale of the battle at the Gurang from Beka. I can beat Ulani to that one!"

"If he didn't already do it on their journey here." I couldn't keep myself from pointing that out. And it was more than possible.

"He would do that, wouldn't he?" Then he brightened. "But Ulani is not able to get up and sing it to an audience. If I work quickly enough I can beat him!"

"Ah," I remarked, "the love of an apprentice for his master."

47. Priests and Gods

FOUR WE WERE, Toare and I, Oorto, Mehetu, launching in the mists that rose before the sun. Once had I feared water, and dreaded stepping into boat or canoe. Maybe I still would, were it the sea, but how could I fear my beautiful A'auwa?

Past Pana'a's fog-shrouded island we paddled and then angled more southerly, toward the forested far shore. "Ruiru has built his shrine by the water," spoke Mehetu. "We could land there. He has added to it since last you visited, Oorto."

Of course, Oorto had spent time there with his lover. He could not be expected to remain at the House of Marareta all the time!

"I would be surprised had he not," replied the shaman.

"Has Hito learned to make wine, as did Master Hoka, Mother?" asked Toare. "We should take some back to Ulani."

"He has dabbled," came her response. "You know he is not much of a drinker."

"Nor is Ulani," I noted. "They like to be in control of themselves."

"Very true," agreed Mehetu. She pointed. "There, between the two tallest trees."

A single small canoe rested on the sand, perhaps Ruiru's own. We pulled our larger craft up beside it. I looked back over the lake to see a couple other canoes — no, three, one very distant — on its waters. None headed our direction. Fishermen, maybe.

Didn't Ruiru come from a family that fished upon A'auwa? I wondered if any still did. Was that a statue ahead of us? No, a standing stone with a rainbow carved on it. Crudely, maybe the work of Ruiru himsef. A modest hut lay beyond it, a luxuriant garden at one side, flowers as well as vegetables, and young papayas towering over all. I think the priest might have spent more time on the plot than aught else.

"Welcome!" came a voice. Where? Ah, coming along the

pathway from the other direction was Ruiru, looking much the same as ever. That is, very ordinary! There was little about the former warrior that stood out. "Welcome to the shrine of Wenatu." He smiled broadly. "And to my home."

A fine home it was, in an open spot on A'auwa's shore, with a clear view of the lake. What matter if it were but a small hut? I could live here, I thought, though Ruiru might object! "I have but come from your husband, Lady Mehetu," the priest continued. "Shall we go back?"

"Are you in such a hurry to be rid of us?" jested Toare. He turned an eye toward Oorto. "Or of some of us?"

"Stay all day! Ah, Lady Rahiniti. It is good you have returned to A'auwa."

"It is, Master Ruiru," I replied. I was not sure whether to give him an honorific but it doesn't hurt with priests. Not so long ago he was merely Ruiru, companion and guard when Teme and I and Toare traveled together. "You have chosen a good place for your shrine."

"I needed to see Wenatu's sign over the lake, the rainbow. The god had been neglected. No one remembers there ever being a shrine to him here!"

I nodded, taking that in. Wenatu surely needed a shrine. He was Teme's patron, as well. But what of mine? "Is there a shrine to Rehe anywhere in this forest?" I asked.

"There is," he replied. "It is shared with that of her husband, Te'eta."

"Sometimes his red dawn shares the heavens with her," spoke Mehetu.

"Is the red star his too? That is also the sign of a god among the Kohari."

No," said Ruiru. "That planet is sacred to Tu."

Still there were many things I must learn of the Mora. I had known none of this. The Kohari had another name and another god for the red star. That no longer mattered to me.

"I would gladly stay here with you," said Oorto, raising his voice for the first time, "but it is best we went on to the shrine of Teva now."

We were all in agreement with that, I think, but none had wished to reject Ruiru's hospitality. Oorto could do that.

It was some distance, by winding ways through the woods and then across the main road. I could see differences. The place was more orderly than when Hoka was priest here. The old priest's wives still dwelt in his vine-clad house, I understood. It must grow crowded when Mehetu stayed there too.

Greetings, embraces, and, yes, wine made by Hito. It was not too bad though he had not Hoka's touch. We sat before his house and gossiped of nothing much. Best to leave politics on the far shore of A'auwa! "Rahiniti wished to know of the shrine of Rehe," Ruiru mentioned after a time.

Hito considered this, frowning somewhat. "It is near but I have never spent time there. I am not fond of the priests of Te'eta."

"Ah, but you surely appreciate the priestesses of Rehe," said his wife.

"What? There are women other than you?"

I fear I made a rather impolite noise at that. "We could walk over there, I suppose," Hito said. "It is a fairly large place. Te'eta and Rehe are more popular than the gods Ruiru and I serve."

We gathered ourselves and set off, southward. It was indeed near, and close by the road. Two statues stood, one at each end of an open space, representing the deities, I assumed. They didn't look like any gods I would have wanted to meet.

A lean young man came over to give a cheerful greeting. "Hail, Master Ruiru." His eyes swept across the rest of us. "Master Hito, is it not? And the Lady Mehetu. Greetings, my lady. I am Mati. We have met before at the House of Arierona."

"So we have." I don't think she actually remembered him. "This is the Lady Rahiniti."

"And you know Oorto," finished off Ruiru. "Rahiniti is a devotee of Rehe."

I was ready to deny this but realized it was, at least in some part, true. Lugan had been my patroness since I was a child, learning the ways of a dancer. "Is Rehe truly the wife of Te'eta?" I asked this seemingly likable young man. I gave a quick sidelong look to Hito. "I have not heard such good thing about this god."

Hito spoke up. "Many of his priests were rebel leaders. They did much evil in the war."

"It is so," admitted Mati. "But Te'eta is a god of warriors rather than of war. He is god of battle and conflict, yes," he said, "but unlike Tu, who is all about politics and strategies, and the domination of man over man. Te'eta is the god of the athlete as well as the warrior. The god of any who strive."

"Yet a god of blood," said Hito.

"Not blood spilled," explained the priest, "but the blood that flows within all of us. Those who would sacrifice a life to Te'eta have twisted his message."

None of that sounded too bad to me. But men ever are putting words in the mouths of the gods.

48. Sailing

As WE WOUND our way back toward the canoe that afternoon, I said, "Gordie does not believe any gods are real. Has anyone truly seen one?"

"The gods of the Mora rarely walk among mortals," said Hito. He gave Oorto a sidelong look. "But Oorto tells me he has seen gods."

The shaman did not say anything for a time. "There are powerful beings who dwell in other worlds and, yes, some wear the names of gods you know. I much doubt they had anything to do with the creation of our world or of anything else."

Ruiru but nodded at this. He must have heard it before but it was new to me! Maybe to the rest, as well. "But do they, um, visit us? Care about us?" I wondered.

Oorto shrugged. "Some do, I think. Hurasu tells me a god has visited his valley from time to time in human form but never revealed himself. So he did not acknowledge his presence."

"A god of our people?" asked Toare.

"No, nor of the Kohari. There are other peoples and other gods." We could see the lake now, through the trees. Oorto shielded his eyes from the afternoon sun. "Ah, Mika is sailing."

I could glimpse a three-sided sail. Any sails were unusual on A'auwa. His canoe was gliding in toward the shore. "That is better than paddling," I said. I was not looking forward to a wearisome trip back across the lake, just Toare and I, for Mehetu and Oorto were both remaining.

Hito's thoughts went another direction. "I hope there is not bad news."

"The taona often sails for the pleasure of it, Husband," Mehetu reminded him.

We would learn soon enough. "Ho, Toare," called Marareta, as his craft slid partway onto the sand. "Your master has been complaining all day!"

"Why do you think he came over here?" asked Mehetu.

Toare gave his mother a look somewhere between amusement and annoyance. "It was just to get him his wine," he stated, holding up a stone crock.

"Ah, of course," replied the taona. To me he said, "Malee complains almost as much. She thinks you should have dropped her at the sacred isle."

"I do not think Gordie would approve," I answered. "No, I know he would not approve."

"Undoubtedly. It might not be a bad idea anyway, before we leave the House of Arierona. You are staying here, Oorto?"

"I am, Mika. A day or two, maybe."

"Then we'll leave the canoe for you. You two," he said, addressing Toare and me, "can return with me."

Unlike all other canoes I had seen with sails, Marareta's craft had no outrigger. Rather, a flattened piece of wood hung on each side. These were folded back now, I could see, but would extend down into the water when we launched.

He saw me examining them. "Those keep it from tipping over when the sail fills," said Marareta.

"Yes, Taona, I can see that." I could; they made sense. "But they look difficult to make."

He laughed outright. "As practical as Hito! Yes, an outrigger is much simpler."

"This is one of those ideas from your world, isn't it?" I asked. "Like Dutsa's barrows."

"Exactly so, my lady. But your world is not ready for this one." With that, many hands pushed the canoe out onto the water and we boarded.

"Maybe they were ready beyond the mountains, though," Marareta said, as he adjusted his woven sail to best catch the breeze. "I left some canoes like this over there. Hito would remember."

"Maybe I should add it to your epic," chuckled Toare. "Such things must be remembered!"

"Hurasu most certainly had it set down in his annals," came the reply. "Ah, you know nothing of writing. I forget sometimes." I did not know some of the words he used, nor did Toare.

But he understood. "I have seen you make marks on pieces of bark cloth," he said. "Maybe I should learn that."

"Maybe," agreed the taona, and said no more of it.

It was much easier returning in Marareta's canoe but also frightening at times. The craft would tip far over when he turned it, cutting back and forth across the lake. For a moment I thought he was going to run us right into the isle of the priestesses. If we were all not killed outright, Toare would be executed for setting foot on it! But he turned beneath its high rocky flanks and arced toward the shores before Arierona's house.

If I knew not the taona better, I would have thought he was showing off. Maybe for Pana'a. Or maybe he just enjoyed sailing.

Malee did scold me for deserting her when I reached the House of Bafa. What Ulani might have said to his apprentice, I know not, but I am sure a full crock of wine would have improved his mood.

49. Night on A'auwa

I DO NOT know why I awoke. Maybe it was the will of Rehe. Maybe it was Ma'ave's snoring. Whatever, I rose and went to relieve myself, checking the sleeping children on my return.

Malee. Her mat was empty. Had she too awakened, perhaps followed me? No sense in bothering Ma'ave or anyone else for that. I stepped back into the hall and whispered the girl's name. No answer. Retracing my way, I saw nothing, though I stopped and called softly now and then. Maybe the porch. She could have been hungry, couldn't she?

A pair of warriors glanced at me and then back to their late meal. Or early meal. No others here. "Have you seen a little girl?" I asked. Shakes of the head, only.

Very well. I must wake someone after all. Pahe? He slept in Gordie's room. I had no desire to worry the girl's father but it must be done. I began to suspect where the girl had gone. "One of you go rouse Lord Gordie," I ordered. "His daughter has disappeared. I am going to the lake to look for her." I turned and hurried away without waiting to see if they did as I told them.

To the lake. Malee wanted to visit the sacred isle in A'auwa, was seemingly drawn to it. She might well be on the shore now, looking out into the darkness. No place for a very little girl to be!

Past the House of Arierona, only a pair of torches now lighting its entry, and on toward the lake. It was cool. I should have wrapped myself against the night. "Malee!" I called, louder now. "Malee!"

And there she was, trying her best to push one of the canoes out into the water. Almost was she succeeding! I rushed to the little one and took her in my arms. "Foolish Malee," I scolded, though there was no anger in my voice. I was only relieved.

"I 'ave to go see Pana'a," she objected. "'Elp me push the canoe."

"Not now, Malee. We will speak to your father of it when we get you back to him." I think she realized there was no arguing.

A man stood near. One of Arierona's warriors? "You found her? Good. The alarm was being spread."

More men behind him, three I thought. He had half turned toward them when one swung a club, knocking the warrior to the ground. "Grab the girl," someone growled. Malee was torn from my arms. A hand went over my mouth.

"Take the woman too?" another voice asked.

The first man looked me over — his eyes were hidden by the darkness but I could see the tilt of his head. "Into the canoe with her. We can't have her raising an alarm too soon."

In seconds, we were afloat and paddling for the far side of A'auwa. "Here," said one. "You hold the little one." Malee was lifted into my lap. I thought to cry out, but knew it was already too late. We were moving swiftly out onto the lake. There were no stars above, the sky thick with clouds, and all was still. All save the regular dipping of the paddles.

Malee, too, was still and slipped into sleep after a time. I held her, not thinking, only waiting for what would come. How long was it until we reached the shore? I could not say. Over an hour, certainly, even with three strong men paddling. Hills rose before us and, off to our right, I could see trees. I knew then we had landed at the northern edge of the forests.

The sky was clearing some and stars appeared here and there among the clouds. Too, a hint of dawn lay across the east. I could see my captors now, not that there was much to tell about them. What tattoos they had were hidden by cloaks and the night.

Their leader spoke. "We leave you here. Tell this Lord Gordie what has happened. You hear me, woman? The child will not be harmed."

I nodded, dumb.

"Very well. Word will be sent to him. Tell him that too." With that, one of the warriors picked up Malee and all three trotted quickly away, as do trained warriors, across the rolling terrain.

I looked out over A'auwa and then turned to see Rehe standing bright in the sky and, behind her, the promise of a red dawn, the sign of Te'eta. To both I murmured a prayer and set off toward the forest and the hidden shrines of the gods. There would I seek aid.

Dark yet it was. I angled away from the shore, to find the main roadway and follow it south. Not so dark was it when I recognized the shrine of Teva and the home of Hito.

"Ah, Rahiniti!" came a woman's voice. "They let you go."

"It makes sense," said Hito. "They couldn't be burdened with her. Are you all right, Tamba?" It had been long since he had called me that.

"Only tired," I replied. "Pana'a?"

"Yes. I felt something of what was going on. One of the priestesses I sent as messenger to the House of Arierona, and hurried over here at once."

"I think they were well aware of what happened," I answered, collapsing on the bench before Hito's hut. More than once had I seen old Hoka sleeping on that bench! Now I wished I could but there were things I must do. Mehetu came from the house with a bowl of taro paste and some fruit, and I gave them my tale, little though there was to it, as I ate.

"We must go across A'auwa," said Hito at its end. Calmly he said this, as a simple fact. "But first Oorto should be told."

"He may have sensed it too," thought Pana'a. She turned to me. "I shall take you back immediately. Hito and others may follow when they will."

I only nodded, rising to follow her. It was not so far to where she had beached her canoe, further south than Ruiru's shrine to Wenatu. I wished Ruiru stood by my side as in the past, yes, and Hito, too. I felt far too alone. Out onto the calm waters of the lake

185

we launched and began the crossing. The sun was rising and the world seemed much brighter than it should.

50. Waiting

CANOES MOVED SWIFTLY toward us, three long canoes and filled with men. Pursuit of the kidnappers, I guessed at once. Aranu stood in one and called to us. "Rahiniti! Are you all right?"

"I am," I shouted back. "Three men took Malee. They landed at the north end of the forest and set out across the hills." As an afterthought, I called, "Does the man they attacked live?"

"He does," came his voice, booming over the water. He sat down and resumed paddling toward the shore we had left.

"That is good," I said to no one. Pana'a and I also went back to paddling.

"It is too late for pursuit," said the priestess. She was right, I felt, but hoped anyway.

I could see men and women on the shore as we approached, and I am sure there were those who ran to the House of Arierona with the news. By the time our canoe was pulled up onto the banks, Bafa was there. "Best we go straight to the house," he said. "We'll let everyone hear what you have to say at once."

And so I gave the story again, to the king and his nephew and captains, to Gordie and all our group. "I am sorry," I finished, "that I ran off to seek the girl rather than wake Lord Gordie at once."

"You did right," stated Marareta "Had you not followed after Malee, rather than waiting, we might know nothing of what happened."

I knew this was so but I felt no better. Had the kidnappers followed me to the girl? I hoped not but how else had they found her?

"Oorto will be along soon," spoke Pana'a. "And other friends from across A'auwa." She paused before asking Marareta, "Did Maratoa feel any of this?"

"He slept through it all," came the taona's response, his voice flat. Weary, he sounded to me. "But he seems at unease this morning. I have not had time to speak with him of it."

She nodded. "Then I shall, if permitted."

"Always," he answered. The priestess nodded and made her way from Arierona's chambers.

"Naught to do now but wait," announced Ponu. "Perhaps Aranu has found the track." None of us believed that.

It was late morning when two canoes came to shore, Oorto and Ruiru, Mehetu and Hito and another. The young priest we had met, it was, the priest of Te'eta. Whatever his name was.

Mati. Mehetu introduced him to those gathered. "The tale has already spread through all the shrines," he said. "Many who serve the gods there wish to help if they can."

"I think we need the gods they serve more than we do the priests," Toare whispered to me. He had come and gone through the morning. Carrying reports to Ulani, maybe.

"The best they can do is watch," said Arierona. "And pray." He peered at the young man. "You used to serve me, didn't you?"

Mati lowered his head in a slight bow. "I apprenticed with your warriors, my lord."

Ponu leaned in close to his uncle. "I believe he was a champion in their games a couple years ago." He looked up at the priest. "A runner, weren't you?"

"So I was, Lord Ponu. And gladly would I run where you would have, if it might help."

"If we knew what direction to run," spoke one of the king's captains.

None of us knew that, nor even what direction to turn this day. All we could do was wait and feel useless, drifting in and out of Arierona's gathering room. Gordie huddled with the Taona Marareta and Lord Beka most of the afternoon. I did not join them to learn of what they spoke but Ma'ave sat with them for a while.

"Aranu!" someone cried, near dusk. "His canoes are returning!" Arierona and Ponu had long since disappeared but the younger man now hurried back into the chamber. He hesitated a moment, before deciding to await the captain on the king's front porch. We followed, mostly.

I recognized the man who approached at Aranu's side. He'eku he was, one of the High King's couriers. More than once had he visited the House of Temani'itu with messages.

"Lord Ponu," announced Aranu, his eyes darting quickly to Gordie and then back to his commander. "Those we followed are gone. We could find no track." He sounded angry, not apologetic. "This one, however, we did find." He rethought that. "He found us, I think."

"He'eku," spoke Ponu. "Have you a message for us?"

"Yes, my lord. One of little consequence from the High King, which I can deliver later." The man paused, forming his thoughts into words. "As I made my way toward A'auwa, carrying Poneiva's words, men laid hands on me and told me I must give a message to Lord Gordie." I do not think he knew which of us that was.

"I am Gordie," said Malee's father, stepping forward. "What have you to tell me?"

"They said you must come north at once, as if returning home, without going to the House of the High King, and bringing only your own men." He'eku had spoken clearly, loudly, as couriers do. His voice softened a little as he continued. "More messages will await you there. That is all I have, my lord."

"Then," said Gordie, "that is what I must do."

51. Separate Ways

"THE TWO HAVE not learned to speak from afar," said Oorto. "They are too young."

Pana'a seemed to understand this. The rest of us could have been told anything and we would not know the difference. "It certainly might have helped things," she said. "Maratoa did sense something of what happened to Malee."

"The unthinking parts of their minds speak to each other, perhaps," felt the shaman. "Now the boy must return north with his father." He looked to the sleeping Maratoa. "I think I should be one of those who goes with you, Gordie."

"I think so as well, Brother," said Gordie. "My own men serve me well but they haven't your skills and understanding."

Ti'ine spoke up. "I would come if you will have me, lord. I pledge to serve you."

"And keep an eye on things for your Kohari masters," said Marareta.

"No doubt," agreed Gordie. "I could use another fighting man. With Pahe, that will make five warriors to accompany Oorto and me." That was when he turned to me. "I would ask you to come too, Ranadi, but only if you wish."

I had expected to go all along. Silly Gordie, to be asking me! "Malee might need me," was all I answered. Gordie nodded in agreement.

"I shall go with you also," declared Ma'ave. "I trust the taona to see Aeta safely home."

"Mouiri and I will be with them too," Beka pointed out. "And Ulani, I would think?"

The bard stated, "When I can walk. I shall not be borne in a litter!"

"It might be faster if you were," said Marareta, "until we take to the river. Do not let pride keep you from what is best, my friend."

Ulani's expression was sour but he slowly nodded. "You will wish to swiftly reach the High King," the taona added.

"And I shall lead men from my brother's house as soon as possible," said Beka.

Gordie had listened to all this with no expression. Now, he said, "If you wish to accompany us, Lady Ma'ave, you are welcome." I felt he was not sure of this, nor did I understand why she asked. "We shall leave in the morning, at the rising of the sun."

"Aranu and I shall follow along behind you in a day or two, as discreetly as we are able," said Bafa. He thought a moment before adding, "We might do well to divide our force to draw less attention. Not a mass of canoes crossing the lake and men marching off. That would be noted."

"You think Gordie's enemies still watch?" asked Ma'ave.

"Undoubtedly." There were nods of agreement to that all around Bafa's gathering room.

"Anything else of which we must speak?" Bafa asked. "Have you business to attend before you leave the House of Arierona, Ulani?"

"I had little of importance to say when I arrived here, some words for Arierona, some news for Gordie. What has happened since makes that meaningless."

"Then let us find our sleeping mats or food, whichever we desire." We went our different ways, not at once, for some sat in knots and talked on in low voices for a while. I chose to eat.

I filled a bowl and sat on the porch of the House of Bafa. The House of Teme and Bafa. It should be so named, I decided. Maybe I would sleep right here; I was ready. I was weary from all that had happened. Gordie came out and stood looking into the darkness beyond the lamps for a while, before settling at my side.

"I think Ma'ave could be helpful if I must negotiate. She knows Mora politics far better than I," he said at last.

"But no one negotiates better than you."

191

"I must do it better than ever before, and I must depend on others as I never have. You, Ranadi, and Ma'ave and all my other friends. This has made me see the value of such ties." A long pause. "But ties to the Mora? I don't know. I will forget any such thoughts if it is necessary to get Malee back. I may go back to my house with her and forget the rest of the world."

"But they will not forget you, Gordie."

"No, I guess not." He sat a time longer before rising without a word and passing back into the house. I went to my own bed soon after.

And rose early. We must be on our way. Little preparation need be done; Pahe had seen to most of it. I need only show up and help paddle a canoe.

The three priests came down to the shore with us. Mati stood watching as we prepared to launch, before saying, "I would ask to accompany you but I know you must not come with too many men. Perhaps I shall join Lord Bafa."

"But Ruiru and I are crossing now," spoke Hito. "One of us is coming with you and one must remain to keep an eye on our shrines and those we care about." He eyed his companion. "We have not decided which yet."

"I suppose we shall have to cast lots," Ruiru said. "I know better than to wrestle you for it."

Whatever means they used, it was decided Hito would come along by the time we reached the far side of A'auwa. Of this, I was glad. Ruiru is a good man and good warrior, but Hito has more wisdom. Gordie could use that. So could I. Soon we were trekking northward with no real goal. No goal except to return Malee to her father.

Gordie, I think, wanted to rush north without any rest, but he knew better. It would do no good. We made a late camp. There was enough wood for a small fire and I still sat by it after many sought slumber. Oorto sat, but a bit aside, showing no desire to speak.

Hito took a place beside me; he, too, did not speak for some time but watched Gordie and Ma'ave conversing of something, voices low.

"Ma'ave and Gordie have become friends," He observed. "I do not think our Pahe likes this."

No, he wouldn't. I blurted out, "You know Gordie asked me to marry him."

"I think everyone knows that, Rahiniti."

"I have not decided. It is hard, Hito." What if I had married Hito years ago? What if I married him now? "I like Gordie. I care about him and Malee."

"You do not love him. I can tell this." I nodded. It was so. "And he does not love you."

That also was so. "I know I could never replace Demba in his heart."

"Maybe no one could." Hito turned to me, seemed to contemplate me for a moment, before again facing the fire. "I think you may live in another's heart. And perhaps he does in yours, though you do not recognize him."

Could he mean himself? Who else? "Does Mehetu so live in your heart?" I asked, attempting to be subtle about this.

Hito chuckled softly. "She does indeed, and I in hers, I think. The lady, my wife, is a romantic, a lover of the old epic tales. The fact that I was named a hero first caught her interest, I am sure! But love followed." He gazed into the dying flames. "We each found a place we belonged and one who belonged there with us."

"I do not know if I belong among the Mora at all, Hito. I have tried to be one of your people, ever since you brought me here, yet I don't seem to quite fit." My sigh was undoubtedly full of self-pity. I could recognize that even as I went on. "It could be different, maybe, in the House of Gordie."

"But you would be the same, my Tamba." To that, I could find no answer. Hito sat a time longer before going to his sleeping mat.

193

Yes, I would be the same, I told myself. I could but seek my own way. Whether it was a way Gordie traveled, or Malee, who could say? Then I too slept.

52. Paths North

DAY FOLLOWED DAY, and northward we marched. East of north it was, for Gordie took seriously the demand that he avoid the House of the High King. Our path only skirted Poneiva's borders.

"This could be the realm of Ruapata. The edges are not exact," Hito told us. He knew the lands of the Mora far better than the rest of us. "As are the borders between Naire and Mahutunoa further north."

Perhaps Ti'ine knew these things too but he did not offer any words. I wondered if he had ever traveled as far as the trade village, posing as a Mora. He might even know the way to Gordie's house from the south!

We could only hope that Bafa and Aranu followed somewhere behind with as many men as they deemed appropriate. As for Beka, it would be many days before he reached the House of the High King and could bring men north.

And ahead of us somewhere waited our enemy, he who held Malee.

It all looked very much the same to me, once we passed over the low range of hills that lay north of A'auwa. Further west, it was lusher, I knew, and there were many villages. Here, the land grew ever more empty, and soon rolling grasslands stretched as far as we might see, an occasional grove of trees breaking the monotony. These were mostly along the streams that flowed down from the still-distant mountains.

It was near evening when two men, carrying the arms of warriors, spear and club, stepped into our path. The apparent leader of the pair held up a hand in greeting.

"There are more men, hidden," whispered Hito. "There and over there." He gave slight nods in those directions. Hito had commanded men once; he recognized such things. The rest of us were most ignorant, even Pahe. "They approach us as the light fails so they may not be readily tracked," he added.

"Or seen if they attack," muttered one of Gordie's men.

The warrior stepped forward. One could see he was a nobleman, surely in service to some lord of the north.

"Lord Gordie!" the man called.

Gordie answered without inflection. "I am Gordie."

"You will come with us."

"First you must release my daughter," demanded Gordie, his voice still restrained, flat.

The stranger firmly shook his head. "It is my master's only hold on you. But he pledges to do you no harm." He looked over our party. "We could have attacked you anytime and slain you all." Whether this was so or only a boast, who could know?

"There was a woman," the warrior continued. "She should come too."

I was ready to step forward but Ma'ave did so first! "Here I am," she proclaimed. The man obviously did not know what I looked like, for the noblewoman would make two of me.

Pahe also stepped forward. "Why should we not take this man as our own hostage?" He practically snarled the question.

It was Ti'ine who gave an answer. "His master would surely let him die rather than give up the girl," he said. He looked at the warrior. "And this man is probably prepared to do so."

"As you would for Lord Gordie," came Hito's words, softly.

Gordie's shoulders almost imperceptibly slumped. "Very well," he said. "We shall come with you."

"Might I come too?" asked Oorto.

"No," came an immediate response. "Two only. So I was ordered." His eyes turned to the rest of our troop. "Continue toward your home. You will be contacted." With that the four, the warriors, Gordie, Ma'ave, disappeared into the gloom and tall grass.

Hito placed a hand on Oorto's shoulder. "It is as well you were not permitted to go. We shall want your skill as a tracker."

The shaman nodded. "Perhaps I can do more than just follow marks on the ground. Malee is trying to speak to me from afar."

Pahe turned to his warriors. "Hito is our leader now," he announced. "Follow him as you would have Lord Gordie."

There were nodding of the head, and murmurs of approval. I realized I was actually the ranking Mora noble there, now, but that counted for little! But why had Ma'ave gone with Gordie? Did she think me incapable?

Maybe I was. "We might as well camp right here," I said, to no one and everyone, "and try to sort things out in the morning."

"That is so," agreed Hito. "Someone look for wood before it grows too dark. I think we need a fire tonight."

I was glad of that blaze, though it was small. It felt like the only light in a very dark world to me.

There was little talk. What could be said of what had happened? Pahe could not even scowl, only sit and stare impassively into the flames. Oorto, after a time, came and sat beside Hito and me.

"Hurasu has also sensed Malee attempting to speak from afar," he told us, "and he says that others are interested. He feels the touch of their thoughts." The shaman must have communicated with his mentor at some time. I hadn't noticed.

"Others?" asked Hito. "Wizards such as we fought across the mountains?"

"Possibly, but he thinks not. They remained hidden. That takes power."

"But they are far away, right?" I asked. "They can't do anything here." Whether these distant — beings might be inclined to help or hinder, I had no idea. Nor did I much wish to find out.

Yet I could not help think of such things as I drifted to sleep. My dreams were filled with much that was strange, I was certain, but all of it disappeared when I awoke abruptly. "Someone is coming," a voice was shouting. "From the south!"

WOMAN OF THE SKY

A figure, trotting toward us, a man, lean and young. It was the priest Mati.

53. Joinings and Dividings

"I AND OORTO follow the track north, as swiftly as we can. We shall leave markers for you to read."

Pahe nodded at this. "I know what to watch for. I will lead Arierona's men to you, when they catch up."

"While the rest of your men continue on the way toward home, as ordered." Hito glanced toward Ti'ine. "What of you?"

The Kohari seemed uncertain. "I yearn to come along with you, now or later. I might even prove useful. But, um, Pahe permitting, I think I could serve better by leading his remaining warriors on their path and being there when they are contacted."

"It is agreeable with me," said Hito. "Pahe?"

"Only be certain you turn and come back to help us."

"That we certainly shall," Ti'ine said. "The Lady Rahiniti must come with us. They expect a woman in our group."

That was true. There was no point in objecting, as much as I wished to pursue the kidnappers. "I shall join your group too, for a while," said Mati. "So I may carry word back and forth. And now," he continued, rising, "I shall run back to Aranu and Bafa and tell them what is happening. If you remain here, they should reach you by nightfall." He spoke not another word but began trotting south.

Hito rose as well. "Oorto and I shall be on our way. The rest may wait or go now. It matters little, I suppose." He and the Diwarna set off in the opposite direction from Mati.

Pahe watched them disappear before saying, "I will stay here, of course, and join the warriors who come." He considered Ti'ine a moment before going on. "Remember who is in command here — the Lady Ranadi. My men understand this and will follow her orders over yours." He slightly bowed his head to me. "As do I follow her orders now."

Oh, I was to be in charge? "As much as I would like to wait for Arierona's warriors," I stated, feeling more sure of myself word by word, "it would be best if we began traveling on and left you here, Pahe." I considered a moment and changed that to, "Friend Pahe."

Then I looked at the men and said, "No hurry, though. We will take our time the next few days."

Ti'ine nodded approvingly. Whether he actually meant it, I did not know.

There was no point in dawdling too long. It was well before midmorning when we set off, following the same path as before. "Sooner or later, we shall have to turn toward the gap in the hills," spoke Ti'ine, as we walked.

"Let us hope something happens before that is needed," I answered. "You, ah, know the gap?"

He chuckled at that. "I know of it. Never had I reason to cross the hills or visit the Mora trade village."

"Gordie's enemies may be more concerned about the other pass," I said. I had thought about this.

Ti'ine did not chuckle this time but my words did bring a smile. "So think I also, Lady Rahiniti. Or should I name you Lady Ranadi?"

"Rahiniti on this side of the hills, I think. Especially so long as you name yourself as a Mora!"

"I may be able to do that no longer. I am known now." The man shrugged. "Perhaps I shall be just another Kohari trader from now on and pay more attention to my family."

"You have a wife?" He nodded. I realized something then. "Kohari. And so would be your children. That is why you serve whom you serve."

"It is so." I think the look of respect that time was genuine.

"Lord Gordie would gladly take one as you into his service," I said, and spoke no more of it. We stopped early, for I liked a little stream we crossed and decided to camp beside it. I slept better that night, though I thought once I heard a voice calling me in my dreams.

Mati caught up with us before we took to our road the next morn. That boy must be able to run all day, I decided.

"Aranu and his men are following Oorto's trail now," he reported. "Or should be. I left while they still slept."

"How many?" asked one of the warriors.

"Aranu brought a twenty and Bafa a few more. Some of his archers. And there was that bard Toare." He seemed to count up the number in his head. "Um, nine and twenty men. Yes."

"Thirty with you," I said. "I did not know Toare was coming."

"He could not be stopped. We all crossed over the lake in twos and threes, launching our canoes through the day so none would catch on. We didn't join up right away on this side either but came northerly in smaller bands the first day."

"So there is a chance our foes do not know any of you are here," spoke Ti'ine. He did not sound overly hopeful about it.

"They will have to find out sooner or later," was what I had to say about that. "Are you going to stay with us now, Master Mati?"

"Not Master," he objected. "I am only a lesser priest of the shrine. But yes, I shall remain until someone contacts you, and then rush back to Aranu. If I can find him!"

"Does a priest fight?" asked someone.

"I do," answered Mati. "I serve Te'eta, after all!" He smiled broadly. "And I hope to fight beside Toare. I like that boy — and want to prove to him I am his better!" He roared now, at his own joke. "A priest and a poet, fighting side by side. He had best survive and write an epic about it."

Indeed, he had best survive. I wished greatly that Toare had been sensible and stayed home, or, even better, was on the road with Marareta and Ulani.

We traveled on that day and saw no other humans.

54. To the Hills

THE MESSENGER SURVEYED our group and decided all was as it should be. "You will proceed to the high pass," he told us. "You know the way?"

"I do," called out one of Gordie's men.

Our visitor nodded. "Wait there." With that, he turned and left us.

"I don't know why they couldn't tell us to go there in the first place," someone complained.

"Being careful," said another. "Wanted to make sure no one was watching us or we weren't up to something."

Which we were. "I'll give him a couple minutes and then head off to find the troop," said Mati. "I hope one of them knows about this high pass."

"Lord Bafa knows it well," I told him. I myself knew it only from the vivid tales of Teme. "We might as well head that direction."

"But how long?" wondered Ti'ine. "Do we turn back to fight sometime soon?"

"I think maybe we should wait for Mati to came back to us first, so we know where to go," I answered. I looked up at the boy. "You will come, won't you?"

"I shall try, my lady." With that he trotted off toward the east.

"So how do we get to this pass?" I asked.

"I can only find it through landmarks," stated our knowledgeable warrior. "We'll need turn more our path more northeasterly to the hills and then east till I see the place."

Unless we are already east of it, I told myself. Probably not. "Let's go."

Our way grew more rugged as we approached the range, with many gullies to be traversed. These were often choked with brush but the hills between were covered by tall grass. At least it was good land for hunting and our meager provisions were augmented with fresh meat. There was no reason not to take time for the hunt; we did not really know where we were going nor had we any need to hurry there!

Closer now, we turned eastward, hoping our guide would recognize his landmarks. "I was here with Lord Gordie last year," he told us. "We came down into the Mora lands when Lady Teme was kidnapped."

Still, it seemed, my dreams were troubled. Once I woke thinking a bright light had shown in my eyes. Other times, I thought I glimpsed Malee in some lamp-lit room, but I could not tell where it was. It is only your worries wearing on you, I told myself.

"There lies the way," our guide announced one afternoon, pointing toward the hills. It seemed the same as the hills we had looked upon for days.

"Then we make camp and wait," I said. "Let's see if we can find a stream first."

We did, for many little waters trickled down from the heights. There we waited but not long.

"Someone comes," a sentry announced. Not loudly; we wanted no shouting here. "Two men, I think." It was near dark and hard to make out anything beyond our fire.

A large fire at last, a warming fire, for wood was plentiful enough on those slopes. "There," spoke Ti'ine, pointing. The men — my men? — grasped weapons and waited.

"Malee!" I cried, not caring if my voice carried. The girl ran into my arms. Behind her came Ma'ave and Pahe. Weary, they looked.

I tried to hold back the tears that came rushing to my eyes. "How?" I asked. "Oh, sit, have something to eat."

Pahe exchanged a glance with his companion, collapsed by the blaze, and began. "Oorto led me to the captives. Lord Gordie, the girl, Lady Ma'ave."

"A camp in the hills, it was, not a house," spoke Ma'ave.

"There were some crude huts, nothing more. I had half-expected to find them in the caves of Momana," Pahe continued. He looked up at the dark hills. "Those are not far from here."

"We might take refuge there," said a warrior.

"We definitely need to find refuge somewhere," Ma'ave said. "Gordie told us to run as far and fast as we could, once we had slipped away."

Pahe nodded. "He would not come with us. To get Malee and the lady to safety was his concern, so they could not be used to blackmail him."

"He had given his word to go to his enemies," said the noblewoman. "Lord Gordie is a man of honor." Ma'ave sounded as if she both admired the man and disapproved of his choice.

Yes, she did admire Gordie, did she not? Maybe more than that — ah, that was nothing to think upon at that moment!

"Do you know who his captor is, my lady?" asked Ti'ine.

"It is Mai'iro, a nephew of Naire," Ma'ave told us. "I recognized him at once and he, me. They realized they had the wrong woman as soon as we arrived!"

"But he is in league with some of our own people across the hills." Pahe spat these words out.

So. I was still in charge, was I not? I decided I might as well act as though I were. "We must leave before first light," I announced to all. "But which way? Over the hills?"

"The pass lies close," said Pahe, "and Lord Gordie keeps a few men stationed on the other side. But there is much open country between it and safety." In his heart, I think he would have preferred to go that way, but saw the dangers. All the more so if some of Gordie's own followers were involved.

"Then south," I said. "Toward the nearest noble house where we might find protection." How far was it to the House of the High King? I was not at all sure.

"Or west, into the Kingdom of Mahutunoa," said Ma'ave. "We are on its borders now."

"Southwest, then," I stated. "We rest now."

To that, there was no disagreement at all.

55. Escape and Capture

"MAI'IRO WOULD HAVE wanted my master to leave by the new pass rather than remain in Mora lands any longer, once he was done with him. I think that is why he had you come here." So spoke Pahe as we trotted away from the hills and the pass. The sun was barely above them.

"He hoped to force pledges from Gordie," added Ma'ave. "I am not sure he would have released Malee even then. It is good we were able to get her away."

"You were able to simply steal out of the camp?"

Pahe answered, "With Oorto's help, yes. Lord Gordie will try to conceal our absence as long as possible."

"They would surely know by now," I said. I had no doubt of that. There would be men coming after us, even if they did have Gordie still. Malee was too valuable a hostage to let go.

The girl was being carried, the men taking turns. Through the day we traveled, sometimes trotting, sometimes trudging. I fear I slowed them down with my short legs. Perhaps one of those strong warriors should have carried me as well!

I spoke of this to my companions. "You can travel more swiftly," I said to Pahe. "You should take Malee and go ahead."

He looked reluctant but Ti'ine seconded my suggestion. "I and some of the warriors will come behind you with Lady Rahiniti, as we can. If someone follows, it might throw them off the track." He looked to Ma'ave. "Do you think you can keep up with Pahe, my lady?"

"If I can not, he can leave me behind," she stated.

So it was resolved they would go ahead, as they could, with one of the warriors as company. I told the girl we would need part again. She nodded solemnly and then proclaimed, "The lady spoke to me."

"You mean Ma'ave?" I asked.

"No, the silver lady. And 'er 'usband too."

Ma'ave but shook her head. She had no idea what the girl meant either.

"They're Oorto's friends," Malee said, and then she was away, borne on Pahe's back.

I had a suspicion as to what sort of friends they might be. Did I not know of the great wizard with whom he spoke from afar? There was no time to think on any of that. "Let us go on," I said, and so we did.

The gap between us and Pahe's little band certainly grew through the day. I could not keep to his pace, nor was there the same urgency now. Perhaps we had no reason to flee at all. We would not risk a fire that night but we did stop, intending to rest a few hours. Not too long!

No sooner had we settled down than warriors burst upon us, out of the night. Many more than we, they were, but it was good to see Ti'ine and the remaining warriors of Gordie seize their weapons, ready to fight.

A war cry from the dark. Other men rushed forward, attacking those who threatened us. Mati, I spied. And Toare! They had followed the track, even as had our pursuers. I hoped they brought many warriors but doubted it.

Someone grabbed at me from behind. "I have the woman!" a man called out. In the darkness and confusion, a hand over my mouth, I was dragged from my friends. Fighting I could hear yet, as foes attempted to join battle by the light of the stars. Then it faded as I was whisked away. Two men? So it seemed but it might as well have been twenty. I could not escape.

Through the night we sped, and the next morning. Near noon, we approached the camp of our enemy. Mai'iro had Ma'ave named him. One man only? I wondered. Surely he could not wield great power here in this backward corner of the Mora realm!

We stood soon before the man himself, a rather normal Mora and younger than I had expected. I had heard his late, mad cousin

Hara'a was a notably handsome man, but there seemed no family resemblance. This Mai'iro seemed to perpetually squint. Perhaps his eyes were weak. He listened without expression as the leader of my captors gave his report. "We could see the child was not with them but we took the woman," the warrior finished. "How went the battle we left behind us, I can not say."

"It is well," said the nobleman, "or as well as to be expected." I might not have expected Mai'iro to be so placid about this. He turned to one of his lieutenants. "Bring out the other prisoner. We need leave this place." The man's attention returned to me. "Now you must truly be the Lady Rahiniti. It is to be hoped that Lord Gordie cares about you or all this will have been of no use. And you, my dear," he informed me, "would be of no use to anyone."

Aiee! I liked not this man's cold words. Gordie was brought forth, stumbling as the warriors hurried him, from one of the little huts arranged around the fire pit. Mai'iro sat and stared at the both of us for a few moments and then shrugged. "Your people will undoubtedly regroup and head this way," he said. "And there is another force approaching from the south. This we know. Not large but inconvenient! Behind it, a much larger one, it is reported. Lord Ponu leads men north and has asked permission of my Uncle Naire to enter his lands."

He laughed. "I fear the old man will know now that I was not simply trying to secure the pass for him! Be that as it must. What we must do at this time is move to a safer camp. Tomorrow morning." This last he apparently addressed to his men for they immediately began preparation.

Gordie and I were left sitting there in the midst of Mai'iro's camp. There was nowhere we could go, surrounded by the nobleman's warriors. Other men, those who had attacked my party, straggled in as the day dwindled. The battle, it seemed, had not gone their way, nor had any been able to continue the pursuit of Malee.

If any of that bothered their lord, he gave no evidence. Gordie, however, was pleased to hear his daughter had eluded Mai'iro's men. I gave him my story, he gave me his. Not that he had much to tell — he had been brought straight here and had remained a captive.

"Lady Ma'ave acted bravely and wisely," I said to him. "You like the lady, do you not?"

He turned to me with a mix of surprise and, I think, guilt. Or maybe embarrassment, if there is a difference. "She likes you too," I stated, before he could reply. I stated this with some firmness.

Gordie only nodded. "It is good, Gordie," I told him, and then giggled. "I think Pahe approves too!"

He could not help smiling at that. "But what of you?" he asked, softly.

"I can just be Malee's Aunt Ranadi," I answered. If he married Ma'ave, that would be Cousin Ranadi, strictly, but I am not one to be strict. "I release you readily from your offer to me."

"I thank you for that, for that and for many things, Ranadi. Far more things than I could ever count." He chuckled. "There is no certainty Ma'ave would want me."

"You two were made for each other," I told him. "I would never doubt it. And your daughters are already as sisters!"

He and Ma'ave were of an age, weren't they? Both ambitious and each with strengths and weaknesses that complimented the other. I could never have been the woman Gordie needed. Neither could Demba, truly, no matter how much he loved her. "Moreover," I added, "she could bear you many sons who will vie for the dais of the High King."

"Well," he observed, "it's certainly one way to forge an alliance with the Mora."

56. Gods and Kings

AGAIN, THAT SILVER flame seemed to fill my dream. And a voice — there was a voice.

"At last! You hear me."

I spoke. I thought I spoke but I was asleep, wasn't I? "Who are you?" I had my suspicions.

"I am Rehe, the goddess of evening and dawn. You have often gazed upon the star that is my emblem."

"Often, I prayed to Lugan. Are you the same?"

"We are not. Be assured of that." There might have been a laugh of sorts. It sounded like the wind chimes that hung on Gordie's porch. "Not in this world, anyway."

Was there a face? A form? I strained but all I could see was that overwhelming light. "Then you do not have to share a husband." Lugan was one of Lacu's two wives. She did laugh at this. I thought that a good sign so I asked more. "Was it your husband the wizard Hurasu sensed?"

"It was. He has attempted to send dreams to guide your friends, as I have to you. It is rare," she said, "that we can actually converse with a mortal in this manner rather than send only images. Normally, we would need to enter your world."

"Oh." Was she or wasn't she really there? "And is he the one who walked in the valley beyond the mountains? Hurasu said there was a god."

"No, girl, that is not his way. I suspect it was our cousin Xido. He involves himself more intimately in human affairs."

Cousin? I had never heard of this god, neither among the Mora nor the Kohari. "So, Lady Rehe, you hope to guide me?"

"There is little need now. As ever, mortals tend to guide themselves rather well. We are interested, however, interested in you, interested in, ah, another who might share your life one day. And you have petitioned me from time to time."

That was more than true. "Another?" I was interested too.

"No names," spoke Rehe. "But we see many thing that might be. Too," she said, "young Mati has petitioned my husband and that has played its part. Mati is one to whom we may speak more easily, though he has no gifts of what you call sorcery." I think her face came briefly into focus, maybe because she looked closely at me. "You, too, are open to the gods. We may speak again some day." With that the light faded and I awoke to the sounds of many men breaking camp.

All the day we marched, higher into the hills. "This is the opposite direction from the pass and the caverns," Gordie whispered to me. "The hills grow higher over here." Indeed, they began to resemble mountains.

There was much time to think on Rehe's words. A goddess, an actual goddess, had spoken to me. Or I had dreamed it. Well, yes, it was a dream but Rehe was truly in it. I thought she was. And I could remember it all. One forgot dreams, didn't one? Who was the man of whom she spoke? One name kept coming into my head. Could he be the one Hito said was in my heart? I had misunderstood my old friend at the time; I knew that now.

We came at last to a high-walled valley and, in that valley, a stockade. Never before had I seen one in the land of the Mora but they are common enough in the Kohari realm. A high timber palisade surrounds the Temple of Mihasa where I had grown from child to woman.

And this too seemed a temple of sorts. Anyway, there were many priests, some of Te'eta, some of other gods. The people along the way gave us sullen looks, looks of hatred even. "Rebels," I whispered to Gordie.

"Are they?" He looked about. "I wouldn't have known but I believe you are right, Ranadi. This must be one of their last refuges."

It must indeed. A house in the Mora style stood near the far end of the stockade, not tall and mostly open, the sort of building that stood in Lanada, across the hills. Mai'iro turned around to address the two of us. "My sometime home, and that of my allies. We shall see you are comfortable. You know I wish you no harm, Lord Gordie." With that, he left us and mounted the steps to the house.

"Has he told you what he *does* want?" I asked Gordie. I had waited some time for him to tell me without my asking.

"Foremost, to enter into no alliance with the Mora." Gordie shrugged. "I was always uncertain about that anyway. Also to recognize — or at least tolerate — an independent settlement on the far side of the high pass and Naire's ownership of that way. He wants to control both sides, I think."

"He thinks to be Naire's successor as king."

"Or if not, to be a king of his own nation over there." He nodded his head toward the crest of the hills rising behind this valley.

"Ruling over rebels and misfits." I had to snicker, just slightly. "As do you, Lord of the North."

"As others have dreamed before us," he answered. Surely he was thinking of Marareta's foe, Nezama. That dream had ended in its dreamer's death.

We ate with our noble captor that evening, a true Mora feast laid out for us. Few others shared it, for Mai'iro followed traditional ways and did not eat with commoners. "Ranadi, um, Lady Rahiniti, has suggested there are rebels — former rebels I should say, eh? Former rebels among your people here," spoke Gordie, after we had spent some time filling our bellies. Mine had been extraordinarily empty.

"I gave them a place where they might find sanctuary after the war," replied Mai'iro, his manner offhand, as though it were a most normal sort of matter. "I am not necessarily a follower of their ways or their priests, but they could be useful allies. And I understand the unrest that led to that war. I understand that there are many who would as soon leave the lands ruled over by the High King."

Gordie answered carefully. "I am not at all opposed to such crossing the hills, Lord Mai'iro. As long as they cause no trouble for those already there."

"In other words, so long as they serve you." The Mora chuckled. "I do not think that would happen."

"Then they would serve you, my lord?" I asked. Very polite I was, though I felt like hurtling a bowl of taro paste at his smug, squinting face.

"I would ask only their friendship."

"There can be small difference," observed Gordie, "between allies and vassals."

"True enough," admitted Mai'iro. "You should know that some of those who are your, ah, allies across the hills have turned to me. They fear your possible joining with the Mora. And, too," he chuckled, "we have spread rumors that they could become recognized as Mora if they became part of a new kingdom."

"A promise that would prove hard to keep." Gordie kept his voice even. How, I know not. He should have a great anger for this man, a hatred, for turning his own people against him.

"I have allies among the nobility too," continued the nobleman. "There are factions here in the north who would not mind being independent of the High King and his ways." He turned his attention a while to some sort of roast fowl. A wild bird of the hills I would have guessed.

A different sort of bird came into my thoughts. "The Owls?" I asked.

He looked up from his meal and wiped greasy fingers on his thigh. "I belong to no parties, Lady Rahiniti." He sat back, composing what came next. "This is an opportunity to expand my power. It is as simple as that, I admit. Perhaps even to make myself a ruler beyond the High King's reach. Perhaps not. I shall succeed my uncle some day and I will be a king anyway. I am preparing for that day."

I was not so certain of this. I *was* certain Mai'iro liked to talk about himself. "Didn't Momana attempt something of the sort?" spoke Gordie, making it sound like a casual remark.

"And died for it, yes. And he was manipulated by Ikataki." Mai'iro now smiled most slyly. "A secret, my friends. Ikataki was manipulated by me. He did my bidding, though he knew it not. My agents, ah, suggested things to him." He shrugged dismissively. "I could not get him to rise to any bait now, however. The fear of Poneiva is in him!"

"Should you tell me such things, Lord Mai'iro?" asked Gordie.

"When you leave here, we shall be allies," came the response. "I need hide nothing from you." He peered at me. "Nor from she who is going to be your wife."

Neither of us was about to correct him on that. I would not leave alive were it otherwise. And surely Mai'iro was debating whether to kill Gordie, despite his offers of friendship, his pledge to do him no harm.

But it was known now who had taken Gordie and me. Had Gordie died in those earlier attacks, none would have been aware who ordered it. If either of us died now it could mean trouble for him. Especially among Gordie's own loyal followers.

Yet, if it became necessary, I had no doubt Mai'iro would kill us both.

57. The House of Rebels

"There will be a battle," said Gordie. "Soon."

"Not if you agree to be Mai'iro's ally," I pointed out. "It could all be avoided." We sat side by side before this house of Mai'iro and his men. The House of Rebels I had named it in my mind.

"I fear to make any decision until I have word on Malee," my companion replied. "I do not wish to lie either."

Meaning he might? "He will wish to fight the smaller force, Aranu's men, before anyone else arrives," he said, continuing his first thought. "Maybe we can get you away during the battle. You must promise to care for Malee if you do and — and I don't."

"You must escape too," I said. "That will take care of everything."

"I agreed to stay, remember?" Would he stay true to that promise still?

"At his camp. Not here."

Gordie laughed rather loudly at that. "Ah, what an excellent little sophist you are, Ranadi!" I did not know the word so I took it as a compliment. "I don't think that is quite acceptable."

But he was tempted, I could tell. "Then the only other solution is to kill our host," I informed him. "You never promised not to do that."

"This is so." He was quiet for some time. Perhaps he was thinking of ways to murder Mai'iro. Then he looked up, as if something had caught his attention.

I followed his eyes. The tall gates of the stockade were being swung closed. "Aranu and Bafa must be here," I whispered.

One of Mai'iro's lieutenants approached. "You two. Inside," he ordered. I could see he was a man of mixed blood, as many of those who served Gordie. Had he been promised the life of a Mora warrior? Maybe even nobility? Mai'iro would probably promise anything — and I would believe none of it.

We returned to what passed for our room in the structure, an open spot with a pair of sleeping mats. A woven mat, with many holes, hung on one side to afford a slight illusion of privacy. It had been assumed Gordie and I shared a chamber. "So we wait," was all he had to say.

We had too much of that, I wanted to reply. I held my tongue. Instead, I asked my fellow prisoner, "Do you think Lady Ma'ave will come to live at the House of Gordie?"

"She would have to visit, at least." He chuckled. "The real question is whether I would go live at the House of Pua."

"The House of Naio," I corrected him. "It is her husband's house, officially." I now became a bit serious. "Both of you would be welcome at the House of the High King, I think. And, of course, at Marareta's home."

"And you will live by A'auwa, won't you?"

"Perhaps," was all I was willing to answer to that, for truly I did not know.

"And Ma'ave and I are also still 'perhaps,' are we not? I shall worry about that when we are gone from here."

Surely the Mora woman would not reject him! But then, I had — and there was no going back on that. The house was almost deserted for all the warriors were at the walls. Where the few women I had seen might be, I had no idea. A shadow approached, moving through the dim-lit spaces, moving from the concealment of one roof post to another.

"Master," came a throaty whisper.

"Pahe?" Then the immediate question. "Malee?"

"She and Lady Ma'ave are safely with Lord Beka, who was coming north with warriors. His scouts came upon us, hurrying south." He squatted beside us and continued. "And then I was the one to hurry back north again!"

"How did you get in here?" I asked.

"I simply walked in earlier with some of the men who serve here. They are very lax."

"Never had reason to be cautious before," felt Gordie. "Now you are trapped here."

Pahe answered cheerfully. "Only until Lord Beka and Lord Ponu bring their men to climb over these walls."

"Mai'iro will surely take his own warriors out to attack those already here before they come," Gordie said. "He greatly outnumbers Aranu's force. And I fear he has more men coming, maybe from beyond the hills." The next words came reluctantly. "Some of them men who once served me."

The familiar scowl returned to Pahe's face. "Traitors," he spat.

"But I can not blame them too much. I never made clear my intentions." He smiled thinly. "I do not think I was sure of them myself. Now I am."

"That is good, Lord Gordie. What do we do?"

"For now, wait. Opportunities do arise and we must be ready to make the best of them."

That sounded like Gordie, indeed. I hoped he was right.

Maybe we could get out when the gates were opened for Mai'iro's warriors. Or get out over the wall while they were occupied. These thoughts came and went in my head. But Gordie would again refuse to escape with us. Of this I was fairly sure, and I suspected it was not just because of a promise.

"I need a weapon," he said after a while. "You have only a knife, Pahe?"

"Yes, lord," came his reply. "It should be easy enough to find some here. Possibly lying about in this house." With that he slipped away.

"You must keep out of the way when there is battle here," Gordie told me. He sounded certain there would be. Pahe returned in a few minutes with what implements of war he could find.

"I managed a spear," he told us, holding it up. "A knife for each of you. The edges are not too good." I was glad he thought of me, even if I was supposed to stay out of the way. "A club in the Mora style. Would the Taona Marareta were here to wield it!"

"You will have to do, Pahe. The spear is probably the better choice for me," said Gordie. He gazed toward the sunlit yard. "We can get closer and see what is going on. No one will pay attention to us now."

Probably true, as long as we did not leave this house. As I stood beside him, gazing out at Mai'iro's gathering warriors, he leaned down and whispered, "Now I know Malee is safe, I do not fear to act. Maybe I will not live past this day. I do not know, Ranadi. Remain safe." He kissed me then, the first time and the last.

"They are ready to march out," he said. "When the gate is closed behind them, we act."

Pahe nodded. I am sure he had no more idea what his master intended than did I.

We watched as the the heavy gate of split logs was closed and barred. Lord Mai'iro came walking back from it with a handful of retainers. I was not too surprised that he had not chosen to go out and fight himself.

Gordie stepped out into the way. "Mai'iro!" he cried out, brandishing his spear. "Face me!"

58. Lord Gordie

THIS WAS HIS plan? Gordie was no fighting man! My own astonishment was mirrored in Pahe's face.

Mai'iro's face showed only scorn. He motioned to his men to take Gordie. So had I expected this to go — until Pahe also stepped out. "Will you seize the man who gave you a home, Bitu?" he called. A man he knew, it seemed. "And what of the rest of you? Will you fight this Mora's battles for him?" There was great scorn placed on the word Mora. "Let him come forth and defeat Lord Gordie is he is a true man!"

A few would yet do as their master had directed but the rest held them back. Mai'iro only smiled and stepped forward. He appeared completely confident. I had watched Gordie cast a Diwarna spear more than once, with deadly accuracy. This was a heavier, shorter lance, intended more for jabbing than throwing. It was his only weapon, save for the flint knife Pahe had found, nor had he any shield or armor.

But his opponent had not been equipped for fighting either. He held out a hand and someone passed him a spear. Still, he smiled. "I shall not kill you, upstart of the north," came his taunt. "But after this you will not be a lord, but my slave." Defeating Gordie so would solve many of his problems. No need for either alliance or death if he humiliated him! Mai'iro spread his arms wide, holding the spear aloft, looking back and forth at his followers.

Seconds later, the shaft of Gordie's spear stood in his chest. The cast had come so quickly I had hardly seen it, Gordie gambling all on that one throw. Mai'iro slowly crumpled to the ground.

"Open the gates," cried out Gordie. "Let us put an end to another fight!"

Any hesitation was but for a moment. The heavy panels were

swung back, conch horns sounded, calling the men to return. That they had battled already, or skirmished, I could see, for there were wounded. Aranu and Bafa might have been outnumbered but they and their followers were true warriors. I could see their troop cautiously following at a distance.

"Though he has led us into battle, Lord Gordie was never truly a warrior till this day," murmured Pahe, who had stood beside me through the brief duel.

I did not care what he was or had become. "I thought surely he would be slain."

"As did I, my lady. It was most foolhardy." Despite his words, Pahe sounded extraordinarily proud of his master. "I should stand with him." Gordie was mounting the steps of the House of Rebels. Rebels no more, maybe?

"Hear, all of you!" called out Gordie. "You needed no lord of the Mora to give you a place of your own. There is empty land beyond the hills awaiting any who wish to go. Only live there peacefully and none will stay you." His eyes swept across the crowd that had gathered below him. "This I promise, I, Lord Gordie!"

He turned to Pahe. "This man," he announced, "will show you the way. Follow his words and all will be well." This was the Gordie who led men. It was good to see him.

Ha, Ma'ave should have been there! She would surely have fallen in love then if she had not already. Gordie was giving instructions in a low voice to his second, Pahe nodding from time to time. Some of these people would surely follow him across the hills; some would not, and remain rebels within the Mora nation. That is the way of men.

"A nice speech," came a cheerful voice at my elbow.

"It was," I agreed. "As good as one of yours, Bafa."

"Better," he objected. "I am no orator." He glanced toward Gordie. "But I should have words with our friend. It is time he and I had an understanding on certain things." He looked at the throng surrounding the man. "Maybe not right now! And I think it might be well if Aranu and I withdrew our men a little distance."

"I'll go with you." There was no reason for me to linger here. No reason for anyone to; Naire would now know of this hidden place on his border and either occupy or burn it. There would be no more refuge in this valley.

"It would have been wise to wait for Ponu to arrive," I told him. "I am glad you didn't. It allowed Gordie to act."

"He actually killed this Mai'iro? In a duel?"

I nodded. I could tell them all about it later. We ambled through the open gate, Bafa motioning for his men to come with us. "Ponu is at least a day behind," he went on, "and Naire is sending men too, now that he has learned what was truly going on here. Beka will take longer than that, I'm sure. Haven't had word on him for a while."

"Do you know if Malee is with him?"

"Ma'ave took her on to Poneiva's house, with an escort of warriors."

That was for the best, yes, but I wished I could hold the girl in my arms right then. Aranu did hold me in his massive arms as soon as he spied me entering his camp. That was the man's way. "Already I have heard what happened!" he exclaimed. "Gordie is a hero now. You must write an epic, Toare."

"Later, maybe," the boy replied, and embraced me as well. "It is good that you are safe," he whispered.

And you too, I thought. "Were any hurt in the battle?" I asked.

"Not badly, and none slain on either side," Aranu informed me. "It was not a battle at all." He sounded at least a little disappointed. "We shall wait here for the others and then all go home, maybe."

"I'll be going to the House of the High King," I told him. I looked at Toare. "I think Ulani's apprentice will too."

"And Gordie, if his daughter is there," said Bafa.

"Yes," I agreed. "And there might be another there he wishes to see, as well." I only smiled at that thought and did not explain it to anyone.

59. The House of the High King

WE DID NOT even wait for Beka to arrive but set off to meet him. "Pahe will handle things behind us," said Gordie. "I have more important business ahead."

His three remaining men stayed with Pahe as well, but we were lent warriors by Aranu and, too, Ti'ine walked with us. Toare came, and his new friend, the priest Mati. "Only till we reach Lord Beka," he said. "Then I shall run back with the news." Mati turned toward Toare and me. It seemed we were often standing side by side. "I expect to see you by A'auwa before long," he said. "Both of you."

"That may be," I said. Toare said nothing but I felt his eyes upon me.

In two days time we met Beka and his men. More than a hundred were they and, on hearing Mati's report and my tale and that of Gordie, the king's brother nodded slowly and said, "So we might as well turn around."

"It would be best," said Gordie. "More troops showing up might upset things." Ti'ine listened carefully to this and all that was spoken, but offered no words of his own. Hidlat and his friends would hear them in time, no doubt!

So we marched south and west into the richer, more populated areas of Poneiva's own kingdom and then on to the House of the High King itself. It seemed very long since I had spied its high roof, the day I had arrived with Gordie. Beka had been with us then, too.

"My master," breathed Toare. Ulani was hobbling toward us across the front porch, a crutch beneath his arm.

"And Lady Pua," I added. She followed her adopted son. I hoped, too, that Ma'ave would come forth with Malee but it happened not.

Pua knew his daughter would be on Gordie's mind. "Malee is inside," she told him. "Go on in. Someone will point you the right way." Without one word, the man hurried into Poneiva's tall house.

Ulani took a seat on the steps, letting himself down slowly, and Pua did the same. They wished to talk? I sat beside the bard and Toare beside me.

"I should not need this forever," Ulani said, tossing his crutch aside. "But it is likely I shall always limp a little."

"Surely that will not keep you from the road, Master Ulani," spoke Toare. "There are many houses that would wish you to visit."

"I have thought sometimes of going back to the lands north of the hills," spoke the bard. "The lands where I was born and was a child. I could leave the politics of the Mora behind, at least for a time."

"Where first I met you. You were but a boy," Pua said. "Once, Ulani was the one who governed the trade village," she told us. "It was in my name, but I let him handle most of the everyday business."

"You could visit at the House of Gordie," I remarked. "You would always be welcome, I am sure. And perhaps your sister will be there."

Ulani looked at me without understanding. Pua, I think, understood all. "That would be for her to tell you about," she said to Ulani. "Although I am sure Lady Rahiniti is bursting to tell you herself!" Well did Pua know me!

"Hmm." Ulani accepted this and went on. "So Gordie's troubles are over? No more attempts at murder? I admit, Mai'iro was not a man I would ever have suspected."

"Nor I," admitted Pua. "He and his allies would surely have desired to take over all Lord Gordie's lands eventually. I think he would have known this."

He probably did. "The threat is ended and at Gordie's own hand," I said.

"But there are ever new threats," spoke Ti'ine.

"Quite true," agreed Ulani. "Help me up, will you, Toare? You will have to remain my apprentice at least until I can do it myself."

"As long as needed, Master."

"Others will need you, my boy," replied the bard, steadying himself on his crutch. "Soon, maybe. Let's go in and find our hero."

"Let him be with his family, Ulani," said his mother. "We'll see enough of Gordie later. And these friends need to rest and to eat. Or to eat and to rest."

I did both, though I would have liked to see Malee. Let her father have her for a while, I told myself. It did not matter much for Ma'ave brought the girl out onto the rear porch after my siesta, as I found a snack to tide me over till evening. "Gordie is with Lord Poneiva," the noblewoman informed me, as I knelt to embrace the little girl. "They finally speak of the things for which he came here."

"Followed by another feast, I would think," I said to her, rising.

"Of course. Tomorrow. Then — I am not sure." Lady Ma'ave expressing doubts? A wonder!

Gordie spoke more with the High King the next morning, I learned, and after came strolling out onto the porch where I sat again with Ma'ave. Malee and Aeta napped on a mat nearby.

Ti'ine walked at his side. "Our Kohari agent is eager to know what agreements I have made with Poneiva," he told us, most nonchalantly. "Should I tell him?"

"I would find out sooner or later, Lord Gordie," said the man.

"Quite true," agreed Gordie. "So here it is. There will be no formal alliance." He looked to Ma'ave. "But an informal one, yes. If you will have me, Lady Ma'ave."

"I will, Lord Gordie."

Ti'ine's eyes went from one to the other. If there was any surprise, he did not show it. "So I shall report to my masters," said he, bowing, and left.

Gordie took a seat beside us. "All that happened here in the land of the Mora showed me that I needed to truly be master in my lands. Not a wealthy trader but a lord, a ruler, independent of the

225

Mora. It was a needed lesson." His eyes returned to Ma'ave. "But I found something else I needed even more."

I was happy. Happy for Gordie, happy for Malee, and even for Ma'ave. "May we all be so fortunate," I told them, and looked fondly on the sleeping children. "I should go now and see you again at the feast tonight." I grinned, I think. "Shall I spread your news throughout the House of the High King?"

"Only if you first tell my mother," said Ma'ave. "Then the two of you may make a competition of it."

I did tell Lady Pua, as soon as I found her. As I expected, she was not at all surprised. "Ma'ave will undoubtedly adopt Malee," she said, "making her Mora. If Gordie is willing."

I was sure he would be. Gordie would see the practicality of it. "But where will they wed?" she wondered. "Surely not at his house!"

"I have an idea about that," I told her, and left it at that.

60. Brides and Grooms

TI'INE HAD DISAPPEARED in the night. It was guessed that he returned to his people at the Great Falls, and would take a boat north. There was no reason to stop him.

"I do wish he had said goodbye," I complained to Toare over breakfast.

"Do not be surprised if he shows up again, somewhere," he replied. "Maybe only as a trader below the Great Falls."

A few moments later, Gordie wandered out onto the porch, Malee in his arms. I had wondered if I should have taken charge of the girl on being reunited but Gordie seemed willing to let her sleep in Ma'ave's room. A room he did not share, by the way. Gordie had made it clear he would not do so until they wed.

Plus, Pua shared his intended's sleeping chamber. That might have been a factor.

He and Malee took some time filling their bowls before coming to sit with us. The girl snuggled against me as she dug into her breakfast. Ah, this would be my one regret, my only regret, for choosing not to wed Gordie.

The only solution was to have children of my own. But that could wait a little while!

"All I have come here to do has been accomplished," spoke Gordie. "There is no alliance but there is friendship and a better understanding of each other. And I have a little alliance of sorts with Bafa now." He narrowed his eyes at me. "Before we parted, he told me about the copper he had found in the hills. And you kept that secret from me all the time."

"I, too, keep my word," I answered.

Gordie laughed. "So you do. I must plan a wedding now before I go. Or have one planned for me, I suppose! There should be a priest, shouldn't there? What about your new friend, Toare?"

"Mati? He might do," said the boy. "But why not Marareta?"

"Or Hito?" I added. "But you really should ask your bride about this."

"So I should. May Malee stay with you?" He rose, already knowing I would answer 'yes.'

"I want to be married by Hito," I informed Toare as soon as he disappeared.

"I think I want Marareta," he replied.

"No, no, he must be my guide when I bathe in the Pool of the Moon."

Toare was silent for a time. "Marareta has memories of doing so, once. He might not wish to revive them."

Ah, yes. Rahaita had been with him. Teme had told me of it, hadn't she? "Then maybe Mati would be a good guide."

"He would surely want to remain and torment the groom during his cleansing," said Toare.

"Grooms," I corrected him. "There is going to be a double wedding."

"Two brides and two grooms, married by the sacred lake. You have it all planned, do you?"

"I do. I only need one of the grooms to agree to it."

"He agreed the first time he saw you." He slid a little closer to me. Malee looked up, momentarily curious, and returned to her food. "But he was dismissed as a mere boy. So now I ask: will you be my wife, Rahiniti?"

"But am I not your cousin?" I asked. It was only to tease the boy, but he answered seriously.

"Only by marriage, my aunt wed to your uncle."

There was also the fact that I had been adopted by Temami'itu and was by blood related to no Mora. I wasn't sure whether that made a difference.

"Then there is no reason not to," I said. "You need someone like me, my bard, to make up for your lack of common sense."

"Do I not know it?" he laughed. "We had best let Ma'ave and Gordie know we are stealing their wedding!"

Yes, but they would not mind. Ma'ave and I would go together to bathe in the Pool of the Moon, beneath the Falls of Pana'a, and stand before Hito, priest of Teva to make our vows.

I said a silent prayer of thanks to Rehe, Star of Dawn and Dusk. Maybe she heard my voice. Maybe she would speak to me again sometime. It did not matter. I, Rahiniti, little Rahiniti the dancer, the woman of the sky, had found what I needed in the land of the Mora. My journey had led me at last to the place I belonged.

AFTERWORD

"Woman of the Sky" is the third and final novel of the Mora Trilogy, following "God of Rain" and "Arrows of Heaven," and continuing the saga begun in the three Malvern books. A third series set among the Mora, telling of the son of Marareta, will follow eventually.

A note about pronunciations of Mora names: typically, all the vowels in these are pronounced separately, even when we have a string of them in a row. Thus Mouiri is spoken MOE-oo-EER-ee. I have used an apostrophe to indicate the stop between repeated vowel sounds, as in A'auwa, pronounced AH-ah-OO-wah. As for words from the Kohari language, I leave you to make your best guess.

Author and artist Stephen Brooke lives and works in an old farmhouse in the Florida Panhandle. All his books are available from Arachis Press, a small publisher dedicated to presenting meaningful literature for readers of all ages.

Visit http://arachispress.com for our catalog.

The Infini typeface used in this document was created by Sandrine Nugue as part of a public commission by the Centre national des arts plastiques.

www.ingramcontent.com/pod-product-compliance
Lightning Source LLC
Chambersburg PA
CBHW030414020726
47493CB00003B/1064